A PRELUDE *to* VERSAILLES

A PRELUDE *to* VERSAILLES

MARK ANTHONY SULLIVAN

Reviewed by Grant Leishman for Readers' Favorite

A Prelude to Versailles: Love and Intrigue at the Paris Peace Conference by Mark Anthony Sullivan is a thrilling post-World War I spy story, neatly wrapped up in a heartwarming romance. In the latter years of the First World War, all American Lieutenant George Murphy saw of Europe was the hellhole and mud of the trenches on the Western Front. Seriously wounded whilst performing heroic duties in no man's land, Murphy found himself in a Paris hospital as the armistice was declared at the end of 1918. When the powers were gathering for the Paris Peace Conference, Murphy was seconded to the American delegation to assist with translation due to his knowledge of French. Although a minor administrative functionary, George soon finds himself in the middle of treacherous and shifting international intrigue and diplomatic waters. When he meets Fiona McDermott, a beautiful young Irishwoman representing the yet-to-be-recognized country of Free Ireland, he is immediately attracted to this bright, intelligent, and mysterious woman with a murky past, a dangerous present, and an uncertain future. Together they must solve the mystery of why they seem to be the target of assassins before they can even consider the possibilities of a future together.

A Prelude to Versailles is an absolute roller-coaster ride of adventure and emotion. Mark Anthony Sullivan has penned this narrative in a fast-moving, action-packed style, reminiscent of old-school spy novels. I was particularly intrigued by the details of the Peace Conference itself and how the major powers were seeking to undermine Wilson's original ideas of nation-building and democratic sovereignty by using the conference as a means to grab more land. The exclusion of the Germans from their peace conference, as well as many other deeply interested countries, goes some way to pinpoint the reason why so soon after the Treaty of Versailles was signed, the maniacal Hitler and his Nazi party were able to find fertile ground for their ultra-nationalist beliefs. Historical fiction built around significant events in history is such a joy to read as it educates and informs as much as it entertains. This story does both exceptionally well. I particularly enjoyed the passion and power of the relationship between George and Fiona. Fiona was a wonderful character who was able to rise above her chequered past and her total commitment to "Home Rule" and a free, independent Ireland was a tribute to the many Irish women who fought alongside their men folk to achieve their freedom from the British yoke. This is a wonderful read with plenty of twists and turns that one would expect from a good spy thriller. I enjoyed it immensely and can highly recommend it.

By the same author

Firebase, A Novel of Wartime Vietnam
Suspense and Romance

New Jersey Consumer Fraud

Mark Anthony Sullivan
PO Box 386
Spring Lake, NJ 07762

This book is a work of fiction. Names, character, places and incidents are products of the author's imagination or are used fictitiously, except for news reports of public figures and other actual media reports.

ISBN 978-0-9990507-2-9

This book is dedicated to my lovely wife,
Marlene, without whose patience and
assistance it would not have been possible.

CHAPTER I

LIEUTENANT GEORGE MURPHY enjoyed the ambiance of the French café: the small round tables, the webbed chairs, the mirrors, the lamps on the bar and, most of all, the menu of the day written in chalk on blackboards. All were enveloped in the aroma of cooking onions. He sipped his wine and settled back. The war was horrible, but it was over. The armistice was signed over two months ago, his wounds were healing and, best of all, he was out of the hospital and in Paris. Paris, the city of light, could he make it live up to its reputation? The Frenchwomen were out of this world. When his superiors learned he spoke French fluently, he was posted to the American Peace delegation, transplanted, in the wink of an eye, from the hospital to a coveted diplomatic position. The post-war exchange rate meant his money would go far enough, but could he really handle Paris? He had always been such a shy kid. Did he have the nerve to meet the women? How would he do it? He could never just walk up to one of them at a table in a café. It was not like asking a girl to dance at a party back home in New Jersey. How do you meet Frenchwomen anyway? Lost in thought, he didn't even notice her until she squeezed into a chair at his table. It startled him so much he spilled his wine. He tried to wipe it up as he turned to her. "You were at the art studio today on Rue de Mont-Louis."

She lifted her face until it was inches from his. "Oui, I was the one with no clothes." She had dark hair and big brown eyes beneath manicured brows.

He kept his voice under control. "I didn't..." He braced his shoulders. "I didn't mean to intrude on you. I didn't even know anyone would be there, but my friend dragged me in."

"That was Claude." She pulled her face back. "We're... acquainted. It's not the first time he's appeared at an inconvenient time with a foreign friend." She added a lilt to her voice. "But you should still buy me dinner."

"W... Why?"

She leaned closer to him. "You were there, and if I could afford it, I would not need that modeling job."

For a few seconds he looked at her without speaking. "What do you want?"

She flashed a soft smile. "Steak frites and some wine."

Murphy hesitated but ended up calling the waiter over. "Two steak frites and a bottle of red wine, s'il vous plait." Turning back to her, "Is that it? Is there another reason you want to talk to me?"

She shifted her shoulders. "You're an American. You work at the peace conference."

"Why would a Frenchwoman care what I do?"

"I'm not French. I am Belgian."

"Okay. Okay. Why would a Belgian woman care?"

She leaned her head back to look at him. "You have heard of the Rape of Belgium?"

"Of course, it was all over the news in the United States. There was lots of publicity by groups who wanted us to join the war, even pamphlets with a drawing on the cover of a German soldier dragging away a Belgian woman."

Her voice dropped. "Huh, in Belgium there was not publicity. The Germans, they were occupying us and pretending it never happened. They still do so now, but we don't need publicity to remember. We lived it, some of us more than others." She stared at the floor. "I am from Leuven where the Germans killed two hundred and forty-eight of us, all civilians. I won't say what happened to les femmes like me." She toyed with the silverware on the table. "After that they burned our library, throwing gasoline on our medieval books." Her eyes watered. "Why? Those books were a loss to the whole world, not just to Belgium. Those beasts murdered over twenty-three thousand Belgians, civilians in our own hometowns, not soldiers in the battlefield!"

When the waiter returned, Murphy took his time tasting the wine. What could he say? "I can't imagine the terror and the heartbreak you must have felt. My only connection with those events were newspaper articles on the other side of the ocean. I may have seen a lot in the trenches, but battlefield deaths and injuries are not cold-blooded murder. But I don't know what you want from me."

She put her hands on the table and stared back at him. "Somebody has to go to somebody. Thousands of people are here for this conference, but nobody listens to them. No one matters but David Lloyd George, Georges Clemenceau,

Vittorio Orlando and your Woodrow Wilson. It's like those four are all sitting at a table playing cards but instead of chips they use people's lives, their homes, their countries. Those with the most at stake are not even allowed into the game."

"You can't believe those four would ever listen to me, and even if they did, what would you have me say?"

She sat back. "You know Hamill, the congressman who is here? You went to the same college in Jersey City, Saint Peter's, no? So did your father. They were even law partners. Hamill is here to get someone to listen to the Ukrainians. The Russians, now they call themselves Soviets, they say they can speak for the Ukrainians. Who can believe that? Hamill knows Wilson from New Jersey. If he can get him to listen to the Ukrainians, maybe he can get him to listen to us Belgians."

He folded his hands. "So, you want me to go to Congressman Hamill and tell him I just met a Belgian woman who wants him to get President Wilson to listen to her."

She smiled. "Oui!"

He leaned back and lifted his eyes to the ceiling for a few seconds. "Well, I guess it can't—"

The woman jerked her head. Her eyes widened at a man who had just entered the café. He was tall with a narrow nose and appeared to be in his midthirties. He wore a well-cut dark suit with a high pinned collar. Murphy glanced back at the woman, but she was racing to the door. The man's eyes followed her. He didn't go after her but glared at Murphy with narrow eyes and straight lips. He snorted before finding a table on the other side of the café.

Murphy had arrived in France eight months earlier. It was the first time he'd ever missed Christmas at home. New Year's Day 1919 had come and gone. After he was wounded at the Battle of St. Mihiel in September, he ended up in a Red Cross hospital in Paris. He was still there when the American delegation arrived for the peace conference. When Congressman Hamill told the diplomats he was an American officer fluent in French, he was offered reassignment. He wasn't about to give that up, now that the fighting was over, thank God!

His injuries had occurred early in the battle. He was summoned by his battalion commander, Colonel Sutton and trudged through mud and water in the trench to get to him. The colonel informed him that their first artillery barrage had been unsuccessful because the Germans learned of it beforehand and evacuated the area. The American artillery needed to fire another barrage to permit the infantry to advance. Murphy asked what he was to do.

The colonel's hands were on his hips, his face scrunched up. "We know the Germans moved but we don't know where they moved to. Once it gets dark, you need to go out and locate them."

Murphy stood straight. There was nothing untoward about this order. He was a forward observer, after all. Although they knew the general direction of the enemy trench, they needed to locate it with precision to establish grid coordinates to determine the settings for the howitzers. But it was dangerous. He had done spottings before, but always from the safety of the trench. This time he would be out in no-man's-land between the opposing trenches. All he could say was, "Yes, sir."

The colonel put his hand on Murphy's shoulder. "It is a hazardous mission, lieutenant, but you should be able to do it. Do you have a reliable radio man?"

"Yes, sir. Corporal Flynn takes care of it." Murphy knew Flynn's family from Jersey City, where they owned his favorite ice cream shop.

Sutton managed to get his pipe lit and took a puff. "Whatever you do, don't let the radio fall into enemy hands. We're way ahead of the Germans on communications technology, and we don't want to let them copy from us."

As Murphy explained everything to Flynn, the corporal took a deep breath. "Well at least it will get us out of this mudhole for a little while."

Murphy chuckled. "Yeah, we'll be lying and crawling in the mud instead of standing in it."

The puddles in no-man's-land weren't as bad as in the trench, and the two men covered several hundred yards before they spotted muzzle-flashes from the enemy cannons. Flynn called the coordinates to the battery, which fired its first rounds. The shots were right on line, but about two hundred yards short of the target. A correction was made, and the following rounds were on the mark.

The Germans must have realized they were being observed because they dropped the range of their own artillery to where the two Americans were. Suddenly Murphy and Flynn were in a raging sea of fire and noise with explosions all around them and shrapnel screaming through the air.

Flynn was covered in blood. Murphy couldn't even see his face through the gore. He put his hand on Flynn's shoulder. "Hey, buddy, talk to me."

Flynn gasped and mumbled, "Take the radio. Get out of here. I'm done for."

Murphy shouted, "There's no way I'm telling your parents I abandoned you on the battlefield." He scanned the area with his field glasses. "The Germans are doing a zone sweep with their artillery. They don't know where we are, so they're hitting every sector one at a time. They were lucky they got us with the first one, but they don't know it, and they're finished with this one. Let's move."

Flynn coughed and sputtered blood. "No, no, no, who knows which sector will be next? They may just keep moving their fire closer and closer to the American lines, right where we're going." Explosions erupted parallel to them.

"Not yet they aren't. Let's go." Murphy dragged Flynn all the way back to the American trench.

Murphy rolled and fell into the trench water. Two other soldiers lifted Flynn. Murphy called to the others, "I've got to go for the radio. I'll be back."

The German artillery fire kept moving, but there was no sign of Murphy.

Just before dawn a patrol was sent out and found him lying in the mud, clutching the blood covered radio, unconscious but breathing.

Murphy was awarded both the Purple Heart and a Silver Star. More important, he received a letter from Flynn's sister, Emily. Her brother was home and told the family how Murphy saved his life. The last line of Emily's letter made him smile. "Rest assured, whenever you visit, you will get free ice cream for the rest of your life."

Murphy paid his check and left the café. What happened? The woman was alluring, but who was the man who scared her so? Was he German? Did this have something to do with her quest? Her quest for what? Revenge?

When Murphy got to his apartment building on Rue Jean-Jacque Rousseau, he looked up at the narrow, beige, six-story building. His unit was two flights up, behind an iron railing. The apartment was small, but the bedroom and bath were separate from the sitting room. Murphy used his key to open the door. The toilet was in its own closet. From there he went to the bedroom. Was there a shape in the bed? He turned on the light. It was her, the Belgian woman from the café. He froze and stared at her.

She smiled at him. "Aren't you going to say something? How about, `How nice to see you again?'"

"How… how did you get in here?"

With one hand behind her head, she stretched and raised her eyes. "I know the concierge. I have for a long time. I can't go back to my place. Do you mind?"

"I don't even know your name."

She pursed her lips. "It's Angeline, Angeline DuBois."

"I'm… I'm George Murphy. Pleased to meet you."

She sat up, raised her knees and wrapped her arms around them pouting, "How pleased?"

Murphy shifted his stance to his other foot. "Maybe confused is a better word."

"Oh, George!" She pronounced his name with a soft G. "How can you be confused? Come. Get into bed." She patted her hand on the spot next to her.

When he awoke in the morning, she was gone. He

stared at the ceiling. *What happened? I never even got the chance to ask her who that man was. Damn!*

He retraced his steps from the night before to a café on Rue de L'Amiral de Coligny with a long orange awning over the corner entrance. It was still too cold to sit outdoors, but the café wasn't crowded, so he could eat quickly. Breakfast was the only time in France you got coffee anything like American coffee. At any other time of day all you could get was espresso.

He sat at a table. This whole encounter with Angeline was bizarre. Here he had been so anxious about the chances of meeting women in Paris, and she gets thrust on him. He had no idea of what this was all about, but it was obvious she was wrapping him around her little finger!

CHAPTER II

AT TEN O'CLOCK Murphy sat across the desk from Commissaire Divisionnaire Emmanuel Trudeau in the Préfecture de Police on *Île de la Cite. The room did not look like anything Murphy would consider a police office. It was no squalid squad room packed with cluttered desks. Instead, there was intricate molding on the ceiling, paintings on the walls, an oriental carpet on the floor, inlaid antique furniture and an enormous desk. In his mid-fifties, with salt-and-pepper hair, the Commissaire kept himself trim and athletic.*

Although Murphy worked for the American delegation to the peace conference, this meeting had little direct connection to the conference. French newspapers were flooded with reports of a major crime wave perpetrated by American troops in Paris. Uniformed American soldiers were accused of committing thirty-four murders and two hundred forty-four holdups. Those reports said the crime wave was so serious an American police chief and his staff were coming to Paris to take over the investigation. It was Murphy's current task to get to the bottom of it. He was assigned by his superiors at the peace delegation to work directly under General William Harts, the American military governor of Paris, who oversaw the American end of the investigation.

The commissaire rested his forearms on the desk. "What is it I can do for you, lieutenant?"

Murphy straightened his back and shoulders. He had been given this assignment because he was one of the few French-speaking American officers who did not work for military intelligence. "The delegates have read accounts in the newspapers about an American generated crime wave without seeing any evidence of it themselves. Do you know more than we do?"

The commissaire removed his glasses and placed them on the desk. "They do not see any evidence of it because the crime wave does not exist. It did not happen. We know crimes were committed by Europeans who wore American uniforms, but even counting all of those, does not come to the number reported."

Murphy exhaled. "That's a relief to hear."

"Do not feel too relieved. What *is* happening may be more frightening!"

Murphy stiffened. "What? How is that?"

The commissaire lifted his finger. "Think of this. Somebody, with the means to do so, went to the trouble of acquiring the uniforms, dressing Europeans in them and sending them out to commit crimes, including murder. They possessed sufficient press contacts to get these incidents reported in grossly higher numbers. Somebody has major resources combined with the intent to do serious damage to your country and to mine."

"Who do you think is doing it?"

The commissaire snorted. "The Germans, who else? First, they send us Mata Hari, then they plant stories in our newspapers during the war regarding our impending defeat. Why should we look for a newcomer to this type of conduct?"

Murphy noticed a photograph, on the wall behind the desk, of the commissaire, younger and in a French army uniform. He was standing next to Général Foch. "How sure are you of this?"

"Not everyone thinks like me. Some think it has to do with the Middle East, maybe involving the Palestinians, the Turks, or the Jews. But to me, it has to be the Germans. They did this type of thing during the war. Why not now? Why would they stop what they were doing just when public opinion is more important than bullets?"

Murphy crossed the bridge back to the right bank of the Seine and turned on Rue de Rivoli. The architecture, the six-story block long buildings with molded corners, intrigued him. Shops occupied the ground floor, but the upper floors were residences with tall double windows behind intricate iron railings. It gave the crowded city an alluring, relaxed feeling.

Since there were two hours until his meeting with General Harts, he had time to stop back at the American delegation offices at Hôtel de Crillon to see if he had any messages. As he walked through the lobby to his office, past marble columns and cushioned armchairs, he heard his name called.

"George!" Congressman Hamill was seated at a coffee table by himself. "Do you have a moment?"

Congressman James Hamill was not part of the American delegation to the peace conference. Instead, he was counsel to a party of Ukrainians who claimed to be the official Ukrainian delegation but was not recognized as such by the conference. Soviet Russia also claimed it represented the Ukraine, as did representatives of the former czarist government, although neither of them were officially recognized either.

Murphy sat on the couch across from Hamill who pushed his paperwork aside. "How are you doing with your wounds?"

Murphy moved his shoulders back and forth. "I don't pay much attention to them. My whole body felt better once my feet were no longer in the trench. It's amazing what dry socks can do for you. I was able to walk from my place to the Préfecture de Police and from there to here with no trouble, so my leg is pretty good. I still have trouble with my left arm though. You know they couldn't get all the shrapnel out."

Hamill's smile was benign. "I'm glad it's improving, but tell me, what were you doing at the préfecture? What does your work have to do with the French police?"

"I've just come from interviewing Commissaire Trudeau. He confirmed the American crime wave is bogus."

Hamill nodded. "So they have you looking into that now. Who does he think is behind it?"

"The Germans, but it's far from certain."

"George, here at this peace conference, everything is far from certain. The only ones who know anything are Wilson,

Lloyd George, Clemenceau, and Orlando, and even they don't know what renegades are doing behind the scenes."

Murphy swallowed and took a deep breath. "How much influence do recognized delegations have if they're not one of the big four?"

Hamill tilted his head to the side. "Can you be more specific? Do you have any particular delegation in mind?"

Murphy blurted out, "I was approached by a Belgian woman who wants to meet you."

The congressman's eyes narrowed. "Why?"

"She feels Belgium isn't getting enough attention, since it doesn't have a member of the big four, but you may have some influence with President Wilson."

Hamill gazed at the intricate molding along the ceiling before shifting his focus back to Murphy. "I can certainly talk to her. But find out more about what she has to say. Belgium has a seat at the conference and will make a point of what happened. Things are not going well for Germany anyway. Stop by my office at the Hôtel Continental tomorrow morning to let me know what you find out."

"I'll ask her when and if I see her again. I don't know how to get in touch with her. She just shows up when she wants to."

Hamill squinted. "All the more reason to ask her some pointed questions before we get too involved in this!"

❧

When he arrived at General Harts's office Murphy was surprised at how quickly the general was ready to see him. The general's desk was simple and functional, not ornate like the commissaire's. Papers were in wire baskets. The telephone was in two pieces. One was a stand with a base and a mouthpiece, and the other was a cone shaped earpiece connected by a cord. When not in use, it hung on a wishbone shaped attachment to the larger stand. The only extravagance was an oriental carpet of rich colors.

The general remained seated. "Good afternoon, Lieutenant Murphy, I'm glad to see you're prompt."

Murphy stood at attention. "Thank you, sir, and good afternoon to you."

The general pointed to a chair. "Please fill me in on what you've learned about our supposed crime wave."

Murphy pulled the straight-backed wooden chair away from the desk and took his seat. He hesitated before blurting out, "Sir, beyond a doubt the crime wave is phony."

"Then why do you act like you're giving me bad news?"

Murphy explained what he learned from the commissaire but tactfully omitted a report that had the general buying an expensive necklace for French actress Gaby Deslys.

Harts was not part of the peace delegation, and his role was strictly military, but as the American military governor of Paris and the Paris District, the behavior of American soldiers in Paris was his concern "The fact that the crime wave was staged does not mean it was ineffective. Already the French people, who cheered our arrival, want us to leave, but this is not a social issue. The target is the peace conference. The Germans are outraged at how it's being conducted, maybe with some justification, but there are others too. The Arabs all claim portions of the Ottoman Empire, many of them conflicting with each other, and the

Jews assert a claim to Palestine. Then we have the Balkans. Remember the war started over Serbia."

The muscles in Murphy's injured arm tightened. Was the general going to tell him to follow up on all these possibilities? "Where does it leave us, sir?"

"Military intelligence is keeping an eye on it, but we don't have the resources throughout Europe and Asia the European forces do, and we don't want to be openly involved. It might alienate our French allies. We need you. I want you to stay in touch as much as possible with this Commissaire Trudeau. How did you connect with him in the first place?"

"I met a French capitaine in the hospital when I was recovering from my wounds. His name is Claude Bisset. His father is a prosecutor here in Paris who has close connections with the police. He was able to arrange it."

Harts steepled his hands. "Another person you should stay in touch with."

"It won't be difficult. He's no longer on active duty with the army. He's studying at the Sorbonne Law School. We still get together a few times a week."

"Obviously he knows about your interest in the hoax if he helped with your meeting. Maybe he can give you some other useful information."

"I'll see to it, sir." Harts nodded, and Murphy excused himself, steering his way around the desks and out of the building. As he looked up at the cloudy sky he realized his role in this mess was far from over.

CHAPTER III

MURPHY ARRANGED TO meet Claude at the Luxembourg Gardens near his school. He arrived early to prepare a list of questions he wanted to ask about Angeline. When Claude appeared, they took seats on opposite sides of a chess table near the fountain. They had a beautiful view of the palace, built for Catherine DeMedici, with its Roman arched windows on the ground floor and the cupola at the center of the roof. Murphy shifted his gaze from the palace to Claude "Bonjour, how was class today?"

Claude laid his books on the table in front of him and pulled his chair closer. "The law school, it is always the same, a lot of discussion, few conclusions. How is your work going? Did you meet with Commissaire Trudeau?"

Murphy was distracted by a young woman riding past them on a bicycle, her skirt flapping in front of her. He turned back at Claude. "Yes. He was helpful, thank you. But we need to talk about something else. The artist's model, the one who was so offended she fled the studio when we arrived, she came to my table at a café yesterday. She said her name is Angeline DuBois and that she's a friend of yours. You didn't tell me this."

Claude turned his head away, tapped his forehead with the heel of his hand and looked back. "It seems, mon ami, she is playing a little game. I have known the lady maybe two weeks, but she said she wanted to meet you and I should bring you to the studio. She asked me to not tell you, as it would make her look too forward. I was surprised at how she behaved when we arrived. It's now obvious she used the encounter to contact you on her own. Otherwise you wouldn't know her name and ask about her. So, under the circumstances, I no longer feel bound to keep her request secret."

"She asked to meet me?"

Claude nodded. "Oui!"

"So afterwards she comes up to me in a café, gets me to buy her dinner and to contact a congressman I know." He noticed two older Frenchmen set up chess pieces on the next table.

Claude shook his head. "I did not know any of this."

Murphy rested his elbows on the table. "But something else happened. While we were talking in the café, a man came in who frightened her so much she bolted out the door."

Claude held up both his hands. "Wait, wait, George, you, you go too fast for me. You have connected with her since?"

"When I got back to my apartment, she was there. She, uh, spent the night, said she couldn't go back to her own place. It's how I got her name."

Claude grinned. "Mon ami, are you sure you are American and not French?"

"Believe me. This kind of behavior is new to me. She was the one who was in control. She was gone when I woke up in the morning, so I never got to ask her who the man at the café was or even how to contact her. Do you know where she lives?"

Claude gazed at the palace and shook his head. "No, not at all. I can tell you she was a stranger who came up to me about two weeks ago at school asking how to find the entrance to the Cluny Museum. Since she was so friendly, I asked if I could take her to lunch. She said 'non,' she must go to work soon, but if I wanted, I could pick her up when she finished modeling, and we could go to a café. When I arrived at the studio, she was undressed and modeling like when you and I were there. Only, at the time, it didn't bother her. When we finished at the café, she said she needed to hurry to board the Metro. There was nothing more until three days ago when she asked to meet you."

Murphy found the door unlocked when he arrived back at his apartment. Angeline was sitting in the smaller chair, but the chair was not what struck him. She was wearing a brassiere sewn from a mixture of powder blue fabric and white lace. Below her bare midriff was a lace bottom, and below that she wore powder blue sheer stockings. She smiled. "Where were you tonight?"

"I had dinner with your dear old friend Claude."

She twirled her hair with a finger. "So, he told you."

Murphy returned the key to his pocket. "You mean about your meeting for the first time only two weeks ago and asking him to introduce us?

She tilted her head sideways and mouthed, "Perhaps."

Murphy sat in the other chair. "While you're at it, why don't you tell me how you knew Congressman Hamill and I went to the same college and that he and my father were once partners?"

Angeline slid onto his lap and fingered his collar. Her lips touched his ear. "Why don't we discuss it in the morning?"

When Murphy awoke at dawn, she was still there and was making coffee in the kitchenette. They shared half a baguette with some jelly.

While pouring a second cup, she smirked at Murphy. "You have some questions."

"Let's start with the last one. How did you know Congressman Hamill and I went to the same college and that he and my father had been partners?"

She simpered. "A friend told me."

"A friend?"

She poured cream into her coffee. "A Belgian friend, one who knows a lot about people."

Murphy took a sip from his cup. "What type of people does your friend know a lot about?"

She shifted her eyes left and right and whispered in a mock serious tone. "People at the conference."

He allowed himself a half-smile. "Why?"

She tore a piece of bread off the baguette. "We want to be heard. We have a delegate here, but he is not one of the big four. We believe King Albert is coming, but all he wants are reparations to rebuild the country. What about the crimes committed? Why are there no trials? We have The Hague Convention of 1907. Is that not enough law?"

"Well, at least I know where you're going now, but who was the man at the café who scared you into leaving?"

She sat still while chewing. "I do not know."

"Do you always run from people you don't know?"

She pointed at him. "I have seen him before, in Brussels. The first time was 1914. He was there several times afterwards. No one I know ever heard his name, but he walked the streets like he owned them. None of the German soldiers ever stopped him. He spoke German. Why is he here in Paris now?"

"Well, he's certainly interested in you… and gave me the evil eye. As far as Congressman Hamill is concerned, I'm sure I can arrange for you to meet him, but don't expect him to perform any miracles. He's having a hard enough time pushing the Ukrainian agenda. By the way, how can I contact you? I don't know where you live."

She pulled street clothes on over her skivvies. "Neither do I. What do you Americans say? 'If my hat is here, I am home.'"

Murphy lowered his face to his hands. "Something like that, but how can I arrange an appointment with the congressman?"

"I will be back here tonight, but I have to go now." She kissed him lightly on the mouth.

"Where are you going?" He stood.

"To the left bank. Au revoir."

Murphy hung his head as she closed the door. Did he have enough information to satisfy Hamill?

After arriving at the Hôtel de Crillon, Murphy was confronted by Richard Ambrose and Stephen Brown, the two coworkers who shared his work area in what was the corner of a salon. The ceiling was painted to look like a cloudy sky, and Murphy's desk looked plain beneath the elaborate chandelier hanging above it.

Richard approached his desk. "Have you solved all thirty-four murders yet?"

Murphy pulled out his chair and explained what he had learned from Trudeau.

Richard threw his hands in the air. "Why does everyone want to point his finger at the Germans? It has to be the Middle East. Look at everything going on there. After General Allenby drives the Turks out of Jerusalem, the British find the city is without food and water. The infant mortality rate is ninety-eight percent. They throw down pipes along the same route the Romans used to build their aqueducts, not just to supply the population with water but to restore the farm fields to their—"

Stephen interjected. "What does that have to do with a phony crime wave?"

"It gives someone else a motive to—"

Murphy held his hands up. "At the moment, about all I can do is keep tabs on the French police. The delegates are busy with the peace conference itself and want me to take care of this problem. They have other things on their minds now and want me to report to General Harts. I met with him yesterday. He wants me to stay in touch with the Commissaire."

The secretary, Madame Hardy, an attractive, middle-aged French woman, interrupted. She wore a long black skirt with buttons running down the side from her waist over her hip. Her gray and white long-sleeved blouse had a wide blue collar. "General Harts wants to see Lieutenant Murphy right away."

Murphy stood. "We'll finish this conversation later."

He was barely inside the door at the general's headquarters before he was directed right into the office. Harts was seated at his desk. "Thank you for getting here quickly, lieutenant."

Murphy approached the general's desk. "It was no problem. What can I do for you, sir?"

Harts gestured at a chair. "Please have a seat. It's more what I can do for you. Did you know you were being followed?"

Murphy grabbed the edge of the desk to steady himself into the chair. "Followed? No, no, not at all."

"Let me give you a little more background. The reason I asked for you to be our contact with the French police was I wanted to approach them from a diplomatic standpoint, and you're with the peace delegation. If I had military intelligence do it, the French might have taken it as interference with an investigation of crimes where we have no jurisdiction."

"I've been told all along to watch my step and not to land on anyone's toes."

Harts nodded. "Good advice. But military intelligence, by its nature, does not like being left out of things, especially when an army officer who's not one of their own is involved. So they decided to do a little countersurveillance by keeping an eye on your back. They say it was not to check up on you, but only to see if someone else was. For now we have to accept their explanation."

Murphy's eyes went wide. "You mean I was being followed by our own intelligence service?"

"It's exactly what I mean, but look what they found." The general handed Murphy a photograph. "Do you recognize this man?"

Murphy's throat tightened. It was the man he had seen at the café with Angeline, the one who scared her. The photo showed him in front of the café on Rue L'Amiral de Coligny where Murphy had breakfast the day before. "I… I saw him once before. sir. He frightened a woman I was with so much she ran away. She claims she does not know who he is but that he was with the Germans in Belgium during the occupation."

The general's eyebrows squeezed together. "But why is he interested in you? Can you think of any purpose he might have?"

"Maybe it has something to do with the phony crime—"

Harts held up his hand. "No, it doesn't fit. The crime wave ruse was well underway before you became involved, and following you would not facilitate it."

Murphy shook his head. "What can I do?"

The general took the photo, put it in an envelope and gave it back to Murphy. "You may need this. Since we now know you're a target of surveillance, we have to proceed by different rules. When you're walking, double back occasionally and see if anyone else does the same thing. Leave stores and cafés by a different door than you came in, if they have one. If you take the Metro, get on the first train and get off before it departs and see if anyone else does the same thing. If you see him again, let me know. Right now there is more deception and intrigue here in Paris than in the whole rest of the world. Do you still have your service weapon?"

"Yes sir, but it's under lock and key at the Hôtel de Crillon."

"Get it back. My secretary will give you the proper paperwork on the way out. As you know, American military personnel in Paris can no longer carry firearms unless specifically authorized to do so!"

❧

Murphy walked back to his apartment. This was scarier than just the mystery man following him. Murphy had walked to the café where the photo was taken from his apartment. In order for the mystery man to trail him, he must have waited outside his building. Not only did he know where Murphy lived, but he probably saw Angeline coming and going. She said she could not go back to her place. Was he the reason? What might happen if he knew where she was staying? Why was she so frightened by him? In Belgium, during the occupation, she had good reason to be scared. But in Paris, during the peace conference?

After entering his apartment, he glanced into the bedroom and spotted her form in the bed. It seemed early for that. Her purse was on the chair. The floor had been wiped. Why? He bent and examined it. Traces of something red or maroon. Blood?

"Angeline!" No response. He went into the bedroom and grabbed her shoulder. Still no response. He flipped on the light and lifted the covers. She was still wearing street clothes, but there was blood all over the front.

He ran back to the door of the apartment. "Concierge, call the police, vite, vite!"

CHAPTER IV

THE POLICE DETECTIVE sat on the other side of the table from Murphy in an interrogation room at the police station on Rue du Colonel Driant. The morning sun didn't reach this far indoors. There were no carpets on the floor or paintings on the wall. "You are saying her name was Angeline DuBois, and she was from Belgium. How do you know this?"

"She told me."

The detective clipped his words. "And when did she tell you this?"

"Three nights ago."

"Where were you when she told you this?"

"In my apartment."

"So you brought her back to your apartment without even knowing her name?"

"I did not bring her there."

"But you knew her?"

"I had met her."

"You had a mutual friend?"

"Yes, Capitaine Claude Bisset."

"And he did not tell you her name?"

Murphy shook his head once. "No, he pretended not to know her."

The detective gave a half smile. "Monsieur, why would he do that?"

Murphy lifted his chin. "Because she asked him to."

"But you met her over dinner when Capitaine Bisset was not there?"

Murphy nodded once. "Yes."

"Who paid for the dinner?"

"I did."

"Without even knowing her name?"

"She left before I had a chance to ask her."

"Monsieur, she was not carrying any identification. Do you know what this is?" The detective placed an object on the table.

Murphy was careful not to touch it. "It's a bayonet for a Model 1903 Springfield rifle."

"Is it yours?"

"No, I'm an officer. I carried a pistol not a rifle."

"It's American, and it was found on the sink in your bathroom, recently washed and dried. We don't know yet if it's the murder weapon."

Murphy placed his elbows on the table. "So you think I washed it, dried it, and left it on the sink while I yelled for the concierge to call the police? Maybe I moved the body to my bed to make myself look guiltier. She obviously wasn't stabbed there or there would have been more blood on the bed. It looks like someone did a poor job of wiping up blood from the sitting room floor."

The detective set his pen on the notepad in front of him. "Can you suggest a better suspect for us, monsieur?"

"Yes, I can."

The officer picked up the pen and began writing. "And what is his name?"

Murphy threw his head back. "I have no idea."

The detective sighed. "Monsieur, you either know of another suspect or you do not."

"I don't know his name, but I do know what he looks like. Back in my apartment is a photograph of him. General Harts also has a copy."

"We will talk with him, but you, you will have to stay here."

Murphy sagged. "Am I under arrest?"

The detective scooped up his pen and notepad and stood. "I cannot say so now. We have not done the paperwork, but please have a seat outside while I call General Harts."

There was a knock on the door, and a woman stuck her head through the doorway. "I am sorry to interrupt you, but the aide-de-camp of Général Moinier is on the telephone. He says it is urgent he speak with you at once."

The detective picked up the telephone, identified himself, and listened, occasionally responding with a "Oui, monsieur."

He frowned as he replaced the receiver. "It appears you will not be staying here, lieutenant. General Harts has already been in contact with Général Moinier. They agree it is in the best interests of both France and the United

States for you to be free to leave," The detective straightened his shoulders. "for now. You will not be able to go back to your apartment, as it is now a crime scene. When you know where you will be staying, telephone here and give us the address. We will see someone delivers your personal belongings there. I was told General Harts wants to see you right away."

Murphy walked to Harts's office. *This is too much. How did I get myself in this situation? This is supposed to be Paris, the city of light. Am I capable of handling something like this? I'm not three years out of college and already an American general is contacting a French general to keep me from getting arrested. Of all the scenes I practiced in French class this was not one of them.*

General Harts closed the file he was reading. "How did this woman get into your apartment?"

Murphy shifted his stance in front of the general's desk. "At this point I don't know, sir. This was the third time she was there. She told me the concierge was a friend of hers and let her in, but last night the concierge said she had never seen her before."

"Have a seat. Maybe it's true, and maybe it's not. How does your door lock?"

Murphy sat. "It's a dead bolt, sir. There's a knob on the inside, but the outside requires a key."

"Was the door locked when you arrived?"

"It was."

Harts folded his hands and gazed at the ceiling. "So the

killer must have left with a key. The police did not find a key on this Angeline or in the apartment, so someone must have taken the one she used for her visits. Did you happen to see any newspapers on your way over here?"

"No, sir. Why?"

"Two of them have headlines saying an American army officer working for the peace conference delegation was arrested for the murder of a Belgian woman with a bayonet they found in his apartment.

"Sir, I've never had one of—"

The general held up a hand. "That's not the point. Somehow the newspapers learned the murder weapon was a bayonet even before you did."

Murphy's muscles contracted, shooting pain through his wounded arm, but he managed to control his voice. "Could the police have tipped them off?"

"Not so quickly, which means the papers' source might be the killer or someone close to him. The medical examiner has put the time of death at about five p.m. That's soon after you left here. It's not quite an alibi but it's better than nothing."

Murphy's hands tightened into fists. "I'm sorry, sir, but I'm still getting over the shock of the murder itself and the fact that someone is trying to frame me for it. I've faced danger before, but it was from soldiers doing the same thing I was doing but for the other side. I could cope with it, but for someone to stab a woman I knew to death for no known reason and make it look like I did it, I don't know how to deal with. Thousands of people will read those articles in the paper. Maybe they'll learn the truth eventually, maybe they won't."

"We can turn our attention to those thousands of people later. Right now it's the police we need to deal with. Either way, you've become célèbre with your name in the newspapers. Strangely, your notoriety will make it easier for us to work together. When you were simply a reserve lieutenant working for the peace delegation, there were some in the military who did not see any reason to assist you. I pointed out to them that you did not request our assistance, we requested yours. Now even those officers who were opposed to your participation realize you may be of more value to us than we are to you."

Murphy's brow creased. "Why, sir?"

"Whomever we're looking for, and we don't know who it is, certainly has you in their sights. We've learned more from keeping track of you than we have from any newspaper leads. Thanks to you, we have a photograph of a suspect. But think of it this way. This Angeline recognized him. He scared her. He may have killed her, but it was you who he chose to follow."

"I'm sorry, sir, but is that supposed to encourage me?"

"What it is supposed to do is make you realize you are at the center of this investigation. I don't believe for a minute that you were the killer, but you are integral to what happened and will continue to be involved."

Murphy grimaced. "As a participant or as a subject, sir?"

"I know this isn't easy, but we have three players here: Angeline, the mysterious man in the photo and you." Harts sat back. "The deceased told you she recognized this man from Brussels during the German occupation."

"She did."

"Someone there must know his name or at least something about him. We're sending the Belgian police a copy of the photograph. However, no one in the Belgian delegation has ever heard of Angeline DuBois."

"She never said she was with the delegation, sir. She acted like someone freelancing."

"Maybe, but you would have expected her to at least contact her country's delegation before contacting foreign officials on her own."

Murphy's shoulders slumped, but his eyes stayed on the general. "I understand, and she had a track record of never quite telling the truth. Capitaine Bisset could tell you more about it. I've mentioned him before."

Harts stiffened. "Interviewing a French officer is absolutely out of the question. That would be sure to create bad feelings. The French police are in charge of the murder investigation. Our limited concerns are twofold: to eliminate you as the principal suspect but also to determine why certain parties chose to involve you in this scheme. Of course, you should continue to maintain your usual social arrangements with the capitaine." Harts pushed back from his desk. "We'll all have to find a way to deal with the situation, but first things first. Since you have to move anyway, it's best if your new quarters were not in an offsite apartment building. The Hôtel de Crillon is full with delegates, so arrangements will have to be made for you to stay at the Hôtel Continental, not far away. We want everyone to see you coming and going. The more witnesses to everything you do the better, and the type of person you are dealing with will be a lot less likely to arrive at your residence if he has to go past a front desk and through a room full of delegates and politicians to get there. Don't worry about the cost. It's covered. This is now a national priority."

ൈ

Thank God for General Harts. No wonder he was chosen to build the Lincoln Memorial in Washington. Staying at a big hotel is the way to go. I couldn't suggest it, not with the cost. Here I was asked to help out with the conference and instead created an international incident. Now there's a murder investigation. It's too much for somebody with my lack of experience, not to mention my involvement with a foreign woman. I'm no international playboy. Look what it led to!

When Murphy arrived at his office, he was surprised to find Claude there waiting. "Mon ami, how are you doing?"

Murphy was planning to translate invoices but shrugged. "Not quite as bad as I was a short while ago, but still not good. I guess you heard what happened."

Claude nodded. "The police have already been to see me. Our Angeline becomes more of a mystery every day, and now she's murdered. It's painful, despite her lack of honesty."

Murphy sat and gestured to Claude to do the same. "I'm trying to deal with it myself. Was she dishonest? Yes, but she certainly didn't arrange her own murder. By itself, killing her in my apartment does not necessarily mean a frame up, but when you add leaving an American murder weapon at the scene and the follow-up newspaper article, something's cooking."

Claude took the chair next to the desk. "What is most bizarre is no one knows who she was, not here, not in Brussels, not even in Leuven, which she claimed was her home."

Murphy raised a single eyebrow. "You know a lot about the investigation!"

Claude squirmed and mumbled, "You know, my father's position and all."

Murphy raised his chin. "Has anyone tried the art studio where she worked?"

"Yes, yes, the name Angeline DuBois, it meant nothing to them. But a woman of her description worked there for a couple of months. I could have told them as much, but they said she called herself Françoise. The artist had paintings of her which matched the photo of the body. The detective, the one who interviewed you, took photos of the paintings. He was smart enough to take one showing only the face, so they could use it to see if anyone recognizes her. He still believes he's building a case against you. The artist does not know where she lived, and she was always paid in cash."

"Did you meet the artist the first time you were there?"

"No, Angeline told me to stay back until she came to me. She said he got upset if anyone distracted him while he was painting. Maybe her real concern was not to have me hear her called Françoise."

It was a good time to go to the Hôtel Continental and see what arrangements were being made. Two pleasant surprises awaited Murphy: they already had a room for him, and his belongings had been brought there, so he was able to have a bath and to change his clothes.

As he bathed, he thought about Angeline. Up to this point he had been kept so busy answering questions he didn't have a moment to think of her. They had been lovers, even if it was for a short time and not of his doing. Now she was dead. She was a clever and attractive woman, if not completely honest. Was he at fault for what happened to her, or was she the cause of the problems? Would there be a funeral? He should go if was any place he could reach. Will she be buried here or in Brussels or Leuven? Did she have any family? For someone he was supposedly so intimate with, he knew next to nothing about her, nor did anyone else.

As Murphy walked past the lobby of the hotel, he spied Congressman and Mrs. Hamill seated on a beige sofa against the wood paneled wall. He went over to them. The maroon lampshades matched the flower pattern on the carpet. Mrs. Hamill smiled and peeked out from under the brim of her hat. "You're looking well for someone who's been through so much."

"It wasn't so bad. I was released after questioning without even getting locked up. It probably wouldn't have moved so quickly without General Harts's help."

Hamill inclined his head toward Mrs. Hamill. "You were a lot more fortunate than my sister-in-law. She was arrested as a German spy in 1914, and it took several days to get her released, even though there was nothing to the charges. I burned up the telegraph between Washington and here."

Mrs. Hamill smiled at Murphy. "Yes, my sister Etta wandered too close to the Eiffel Tower, not realizing it had become a restricted area. She thought it was a tourist site like before the war. She wouldn't have made much of a spy. Fortunately Jim was able to straighten it out. It was scary to think back on it after what they did to Mata Hari, shooting her. It's chilling to think my sister was held under similar circumstances."

They were interrupted by the arrival of a French couple. Hamill stood and placed his hand on Murphy's shoulder. "May I present Lieutenant George Murphy, an army officer working with the peace delegation."

The woman gaped at Murphy and shouted, "You, you're the one who killed the poor Belgian girl. What are you doing here? Why are you not still in jail?" She scowled at Hamill and stormed out of the room, followed by her husband.

Hamill spoke louder than necessary to make sure anyone who had heard Madame's outburst would hear him. "There are no charges against Lieutenant Murphy, and, other than the fact the body was found in his apartment, the evidence all points to someone else. There are certain newspapers trying to create a nonexistent American crime wave. You can't believe what you read in their articles. They knew the murder weapon was a bayonet even before Lieutenant Murphy and the police did." He invited Murphy to sit in one of the chairs.

Murphy took the seat but looked at the floor. *I did it again. I upset the Hamills after they were so nice to me.*

Mrs. Hamill tilted her head to Murphy and whispered, "You can't blame yourself for this, George. Someone is obviously trying to set you up. You're a victim here."

Murphy forced a smile. "Thank you, Mrs. Hamill. The past year and a half are the first time I've ever been away from home, and I feel like I'm messing things up. Why couldn't I have tried something closer, like New York or Washington, before attempting Paris?"

As he rose to leave, an army officer nearby stood, walked over and offered his hand to Murphy. He wore an unusual combination of an Arab headdress over a British uniform. "Lieutenant Murphy, I'm Colonel Lawrence. I may not know what happened in your apartment, but it's clear the whole string of newspaper articles are nothing but rubbish. The facts, whatever they may be, should stand on their own merit."

"Thank you, sir."

Lawrence nodded. "Congressman, Mrs. Hamill." He smiled at Murphy before returning to his companions.

Hamill patted Murphy on the arm. "That was Lawrence of Arabia, no less! He and I have something in common. Although he's British, he's here on behalf of another unrecognized delegation. In his case the Saudi one."

CHAPTER V

THE FOLLOWING AFTERNOON as Murphy rode the elevator to the lobby of the Continental the man next to him spoke with a German accent. "You are Lieutenant Murphy, is that not so?"

Murphy lifted his eyes. The man appeared to be in his forties, short, and muscular, and his hair was dark and cut close. "That's correct, and you are?"

The man carried a coat over his arm. "Major Muller. I am an officer in the German army. Unfortunately, I cannot wear my uniform here. These French are inclined to throw things at German soldiers despite the armistice."

They reached the ground floor and stepped out. Murphy turned to the major. "Is there something you have on your mind?"

"Yes, I want to assure you our delegation is not behind the accusation that you killed the Belgian girl. We do not know who did, nor do we recognize the photograph of the man who was following you. It was shown to us by the French police."

Murphy's eyes widened. "How can you know what someone else might or might not have done? I'm sure such things would never be discussed at a round table."

"If someone in our delegation did it, I would learn about it. Any attempt to conceal it would be useless. More to the point, if the man in the photograph were one of ours, I would know who he was, and I do not."

Murphy picked a newspaper up from a table. "Were you in Belgium during the occupation?"

"No, but I was at St. Mihiel when you were wounded. We may have exchanged fire with each other."

"Maybe you were responsible for the round that hit me."

Muller swung his coat over his shoulders. "It would be unfortunate but often unavoidable in war. But now there is an armistice, an armistice based on your President Wilson's Fourteen Points. The fourteen points no one is adhering to. Our delegation has not even been allowed a seat at the conference."

"You're not the only one. Ireland, the Ukraine, and Armenia were denied seats as well, and they were not warring parties. Lots of people are unhappy."

"What you say is true but remember, the real purpose of this conference is to establish a lasting peace." The major buttoned his coat. "Do you think it will succeed in doing so?"

Murphy blinked. "Not without divine intervention!"

❧

As Murphy shuffled by the front desk, the receptionist called out to him. "Congressman Hamill asks for you to see him in his chamber."

Murphy waved. "Merci."

Two people were with the congressman. One was a man who appeared to be older with a narrow face and combed-back dark hair graying at the edges. With his suit and tie he wore a wing-tipped collar, but it was the other person who grabbed Murphy's attention. It was hard to take his eyes off her. Her wide hat covered most of her dark blond hair. Her dress had natural shoulders and a tight waist. She had gorgeous deep blue eyes that stared right through him.

Hamill stood. "Mr. O'Kelly, Miss McDermott, allow me to introduce Lieutenant George Murphy. He was wounded at St. Mihiel and is now working for the American delegation. George, this is Mr. Sean O'Kelly, Ireland's proposed chief delegate to the peace conference, and this is Miss Fiona McDermott, a member of the delegation."

Murphy mumbled, "Pleased to meet you."

O'Kelly stood and held out his hand. "And I you."

Miss McDermott rolled her eyes. "Of course, I'm so delighted to meet you."

Murphy took the hand, and O'Kelly smiled. "Please do not think us dreamers, lieutenant. We understand full well the difficulties we are facing, as are the Ukraine, Armenia, and Indochina. Even recognized delegations may not be able to affect the outcome of this conference, which will be determined by the big four, including Lloyd George, but we want to make our presence known. Ireland will assume its rightful place among nations, just not today, but the citizens of other countries must become accustomed to seeing us on the world stage if we are to establish the credibility we will need when our time comes. Can you understand?"

"You sound practical." They both took their seats. "Of

course, I understand, but what can I do? If you sold supplies to the delegation and submitted an invoice in French, I could make sure you got paid, but no one asks my advice on seating delegations."

"What I was hoping you would do is to take Fiona here for a tour of your office and take her for lunch there at the Hôtel de Crillon. No one would think it unusual for a young man to be showing a young woman where he worked. Introduce her to your friends there and tell them why she's here. It will help make our presence known."

"Okay, I'm sure I can do that."

She glared at him. "Aren't I blessed?"

O'Kelly smirked. "Don't worry. She does have good diplomatic skills when they're needed."

Murphy nodded. "Of course." But could he make it through a whole meal with this woman?

O'Kelly arranged for Fiona to arrive at Murphy's office at the Hôtel de Crillon around eleven o'clock Saturday morning. Her clothes were different from what she wore the day before. Her dress was reddish in color and tight, not only at the waist, but almost all the way to her ankles. *Time to go to work. What will George Murphy think of me this time?*

She entered the room with a glowing smile, her eyes fixed on him. "Oh, George, I did not realize how beautiful this place was. I have never seen such gorgeous ceiling art."

Since Richard and Stephen were both gawking at her, Murphy introduced them. "Fiona, this is Stephen Brown, and this is Richard Ambrose. Stephen oversees scheduling meetings and reserving a place to hold them. Richard takes care of travel arrangements. Stephen and Richard, this is Fiona McDermott. She's with the Irish delegation."

Fiona gave them a wide smile. "George, you did not tell me how handsome your coworkers were." She tucked her head slightly and glanced at Murphy from the corner of her eye. "If you had, I would have come sooner."

Murphy snickered. "I didn't tell you because I never noticed, but I'll take your word for it."

Fiona offered her hand to Stephen. "Stephen, your work must be exiting, setting schedules for meetings of all of those important people. You must be sharp to keep track all their comings and goings."

Stephen blinked. "Well, it sure keeps me busy. I will say so, miss."

"Stephen please, it's Fiona." She offered her hand to Richard. "And you, Richard, to be responsible for the travel plans of the most important diplomats in the world. It must be stimulating."

Richard took her hand but released it quickly. "Thank you… Fiona. How is your delegation doing?"

"No one is inclined to seat us, but we're not leaving, so they better get used to us!"

After the office tour concluded, Murphy and Fiona proceeded to the hotel restaurant where they sat in cushioned armchairs on opposite sides of a table covered with a white tablecloth that almost touched the floor. Murphy ordered a glass of red Bordeaux for himself and a glass of white Burgundy for Fiona. In a low voice, he murmured, "Who are you, and what have you done with the woman I met yesterday?"

She laughed, reached across and squeezed his arm. "Oh, George, relax. We're old friends now."

When the waiter came, Murphy ordered the grilled duck with turnips and caramelized beets for himself. For Fiona, he ordered the veal sweetbreads with glazed parsnips tangerine.

The waiter left, but Murphy's eyes widened as General Tasker Bliss made his way to their table. Murphy snapped to his feet, but the general put a hand on his shoulder. "Lieutenant Murphy, I wanted to thank you for establishing the crime wave was a hoax. Keep up your contacts. There's more we need to know." He smiled at Fiona. "Who is your charming companion?"

After introducing them, Murphy said, "Miss McDermott is part of the unrecognized Irish delegation."

General Bliss gave a small bow. "Nice to meet you, miss. I can't say you'll have much luck, not with Lloyd George being one of the big four, but it's a pleasure to have you here."

Her white teeth gleamed as she smiled. "Thank you, general. I am honored. I recall it was you who commanded the American army during the Moro Rebellion in the Philippines."

General Bliss laughed. "Lieutenant Murphy, be sure to keep this woman around. She knows a thing or two."

Murphy grinned. "Yes, sir. Thank you."

After Bliss left, Murphy sat and muttered, "How did you know that?"

She whispered, "It's my job to come prepared with information."

As Fiona finished her sweetbreads Ambassador Henry White approached their table. "Good afternoon, Lieutenant Murphy. I hope the confusion about the Belgian girl gets cleared up soon. I hope it's not too harrowing."

Murphy stood. "No, it isn't. Thank you, sir. May I introduce Miss Fiona McDermott? She is part of the delegation sent here by the provisional government of Ireland, even though it's not officially recognized."

Ambassador White smiled at Fiona. "It's a pleasure to meet you, Miss McDermott. I can't imagine you ever not being recognized."

"And I am honored to meet you. I've been told you are the most experienced diplomat here, having been ambassador to both France and Italy. I understand you introduced former President Roosevelt to all the heads of state of Europe."

"All except the czar but thank you for the compliment." He nodded and went back to his own table.

Fiona flickered a smile at Murphy. "You know some important people."

"I may know them, but not well. They would never have bothered coming to this table were it not for you. If President Wilson arrives and comes over to greet us, I'll just keep my mouth shut and let you take over. How did you acquire all this savoir-faire, anyway?"

She lowered her head but kept her eyes on him. "I may tell you someday, but today is not that day!"

As she walked back to her hotel, Fiona grinned to herself. *I've met two top diplomats who won't forget me or that I represent the provisional government of Ireland. And I've done something to smooth things over with George Murphy, … but not too much, not so much that he won't still regard me with caution. A girl in my situation can't afford to let her guard down, but it's nice he didn't brag. He didn't try to impress me with how important he was the way most men do.*

CHAPTER VI

THE FOLLOWING THURSDAY, when Murphy finished his work, he walked along Rue de Rivoli, passed his hotel and continued to the gilded statue of Joan of Arc on horseback, holding her banner. He circled the monument, pretended to study it and went back the other way. Using a tobacco store window as a mirror, he saw a man in a large overcoat do the same thing.

A voice at the door said, "Good evening, lieutenant."

Murphy turned his head. "Major Muller, to what do I owe this pleasure?"

Muller straightened his hat. "It's not a question of pleasure, lieutenant. The future of the world depends on what we do here at this conference."

Murphy gave a tight smile. "So, as long as I translate invoices well enough the world will enjoy everlasting peace?"

Muller's smile was sardonic. "We all know you do more than that."

Murphy gestured toward the street. "Is the man following me in the great overcoat one of yours?"

Muller threw his head back and grinned. "No, he's from your own military intelligence. He's probably the same one who took the photograph of your mystery man."

Murphy paused before conceding, "That does make sense."

"If we were to conduct such an operation, there would have been two men, one following you and one following him, but too far back for you to see. If you had turned around, the first one would have kept on walking but would have given the second a subtle signal, like taking his hat off and holding it in his hand. The following man would then stop and wait for you to go by before trailing behind you. You would not see anyone turn around after you."

Murphy stared. "How did you know what happened?"

"I watched you both go by from inside the store." He gave a polite nod. "I have to meet someone for dinner, so I must leave."

"Bon appetit." Murphy continued back toward his hotel. The sidewalk along Rue de Rivoli was an arcade with a roof over it supported by multiple Roman arches. It gave the whole street an elegant appearance. He had barely turned from the store when another man stepped in front of him, stopped and stared him in the face. He was medium height and slim with a narrow face. His hair was long and poorly combed. He wore a disheveled jacket and a loose tie.

Murphy frowned. "Who are you?"

"Henri Durand, reporter for *Paris Aujourd'hui.* Why are you not in jail?"

Murphy's hands were on his hips. "Because I was never arrested. It would have taken an Olympic marathon champion to get from General Harts's office to my apartment in time to kill the victim. Also, your newspaper knew more about the crime than the police. Who told you the murder weapon was a bayonet?"

The man took out a pencil. "Monsieur, you are not the one who gets to ask questions."

Murphy resumed walking. "Nor are you."

"No? Does your wife in New Jersey know about your affair with Mademoiselle DuBois?"

Murphy stopped dead in his tracks. "Wife? I've never been married."

Durand smiled. "See how easy it is to get you to talk. Tell me what happened between you and Mademoiselle DuBois, and I will print your version. Otherwise I will have to print what my other sources tell me."

Murphy tried to go around him. "Go to Hell!"

"I understand she was pregnant with your child."

Murphy hurried along. "It's impossible. We only met two days before."

"Thank you, but she had already moved into your apartment?"

&

On entering Hôtel Continental Murphy did not turn right toward the elevators. Instead he went left to the bar, sat in a leather chair at a table and ordered a whiskey. He had just taken a sip when a tall man in a trench coat approached him and spoke in an English accent. "Lieutenant Murphy, I'm Major Bennett from MI5. Do you mind if I join you for a few minutes?"

Murphy observed the man had a guard mustache. "MI5, isn't that an intelligence organization?"

The man's stance was rigid. "Counterintelligence. We're affiliated with the Home Office."

Murphy waved his hand. "You can join me for a little while. I have to meet someone for dinner."

The man took a chair. "Not Fiona McDermott, I hope."

Murphy stiffened. "No, but why is it any concern of yours?"

Bennett sat back. "Everything Fiona McDermott does is of concern to us. She works with Michael Collins and the so-called provisional government in Ireland. Collins was elected to the British Parliament and could be sitting in Westminster if he chose. Instead he and his chums claim to have established their own parliament. They have no business sending delegates to this conference, let alone someone like her."

Murphy continued to sit as straight as an arrow. "Neither you nor I get to make that decision. If it's any consolation, their chances of getting seated are close to zero. They just want the world to know they're willing to do their part, but what do you mean by, 'someone like her?'"

Bennett chuckled. "I'm sure you'll learn soon enough."

Murphy spat back, "What does counterintelligence have to do with any of this?"

"They may be engaging in diplomacy now, but the Irish are never far from violent rebellion. Look at what happened at Eastertime three years ago."

"Which would have been a victory for you if you hadn't executed the leaders. All that did was to turn the world against you for violently suppressing a freedom movement. It had the same effect on many Irish who had been sitting on the fence."

The man snarled, "Armed rebellion is never the way to go."

Murphy smirked. "What do you think of George Washington?"

Bennett's face sagged. "We're not making any progress here, but I want to make sure you realize it was a mistake to introduce her to the leaders of your delegation."

"You're not having much success."

"Look here, I'm trying to be nice about this. There are people here in Paris who will not be. There are groups from Belfast who can be as violent as the IRA."

"Shouldn't you counterintelligence people be doing something about them?"

His nose and mouth were scrunched up as he snarled, "We can try, but our resources here are limited."

"But not so limited you can't expend them on an unarmed young woman."

"Miss McDermott would be a lot safer if she kept a lower profile."

Murphy pointed his index finger back at the man. "I haven't known her long, but I've known her long enough to know she would never agree."

"Maybe not, but don't say I didn't warn you." Bennett bolted for the door.

As Murphy watched him, someone else left as well, from a different table, that pesky reporter Henri Durand!

ঌ

As soon as he arrived at his office Friday, Murphy was told Ambassador White wanted to see him. He was shown into the office, and the ambassador rose and shook his hand. "It was a pleasure to meet your friend Miss McDermott last week, but I should let you know there's been some grumbling."

"I suspect it's from the British, sir. An MI5 officer confronted me yesterday about my bringing her here."

White sat and gestured to Murphy to do the same. "The grumbling is from the British. Someone in their delegation was in the hotel restaurant when General Bliss and I met her. By the time the story got back to the diplomats at the Majestic Hôtel, it had us conducting a formal meeting and negotiating with her." He held up his hand. "Don't worry, I cleared up any misunderstandings. They now know our purpose was to speak with you and she was there only as your guest." White paused. "But MI5, strange!"

"The officer called himself Major Bennett and went well beyond expressing his government's displeasure. He warned me there was a group here from Belfast that could resort to violence."

The ambassador sat ramrod straight. "A threat! It's good you told me. We can't ignore it, when it was made to one of our people. MI5 would never do anything so offensive. Something else is at work. I will make sure General Harts is made aware of it. He can pass it on to Général Moinier and Commissaire Trudeau. I will also see that British security is notified!"

Murphy returned to his desk and found a message from Sean O'Kelly saying he was in the Crillon lobby and asking Murphy to meet him there.

O'Kelly was seated on a curved leather sofa under a grand chandelier. There was a round marble table looking out on the courtyard. "It was good of you to come. Thank you for introducing Fiona around. I understand she met two of your top delegates."

Murphy took a seat halfway around the couch. "Yes, and they were quite taken with her."

"Everyone gets taken with Fiona, sometimes too much so."

Murphy's head jerked. "I think I know what you mean." He went on to tell him about his encounter with Bennett the day before, including the threat. "He referred to Fiona derogatively as 'someone like her.'"

O'Kelly looked away for a few seconds before responding, "George, Fiona comes from a complex background. I'm not free to talk about it now, but there are targets more central to the mission of the Irish delegation, myself, for example. There must be a reason why they chose Fiona, and the reason may depend on who they turn out to be. I don't recognize Major Bennett's name, and I usually would with those people. What did he look like?"

"Tall, slim, late forties, thinning hair, guard-type mustache."

"Appearances aside, his actions do not sound like MI5 at all. The British Foreign Ministry would not take kindly to anyone from a counterintelligence organization admonishing staff of a foreign diplomatic delegation, let alone threatening one."

Murphy rested against the cushioned back. "Any thoughts about who it might be?"

O'Kelly shook his head. "I have not any for certain,

but the Germans would like to make a point to the Americans that the British are not acting in accord with Wilson's Fourteen Points, which everyone was told was the basis for the armistice."

Murphy lifted his chin. "So you think Bennett`s English accent might be faked?"

O'Kelly half-smiled. "I will not say it is. I will not say it is not, but, in either event, Fiona should be made aware of this. She never backs off from anything, but she needs to keep her eyes open."

CHAPTER VII

AFTER WORK, AS Murphy walked by the Hôtel Continental lobby, he spotted Fiona seated on a couch chatting with two other women. He walked right over. "Good evening, Fiona. How are you feeling?"

As she looked up, the brim of her hat tilted back. "Me, I'm quite fine. Is there any reason I shouldn't be?"

"Have you spoken with Mr. O'Kelly?"

"If you mean did he tell me about the threat some strange person made to you about me, yes."

"I didn't want to upset you, but you had to know about it."

She pressed her folded hands into her lap and edged her shoulders forward. "George, it would be a bigger shock if the threats against me were to stop." She straightened up and introduced Murphy to the other women. The older of the two was a baroness.

Murphy gave a slight bow. "A pleasure to meet you ladies."

The baroness offered Murphy her hand. "Enchanté, lieutenant. You may have noticed we are the only women in the room who are not employees of the hotel. We are working here with the Y.W.C.A. because it is all we have left. Would you know of any empty delegates' seats we could occupy?"

Murphy smirked. "I don't even know of any I could occupy. My position is not so high."

She smiled at him. "Someone so low doesn't usually get his name in the newspapers."

"Nor do I for anything good."

The baroness waved her hand. "Do not worry yourself. I don't take you for a murderer."

"As Fiona may have told you, even though I can't do anything about getting her delegation seated, I did introduce her to some of our senior people."

The baroness's hands were pressed flat above her chest below her throat. "She told us. Is that what these threats are about?"

Murphy shifted his weight to his good leg. "They are. Fiona's recent activities are a big factor. But, like you said when we were first introduced, you want to play a bigger part in what is going on." He gestured at Fiona. "Fiona chose her role and would be more upset than she is now if I refused to cooperate." Fiona dropped her head concealing the smile on her face.

The baroness glanced at Fiona and back at Murphy. "I am not suggesting you should not have done it, lieutenant, but you are already deeply involved in Mademoiselle McDermott's present situation, too involved to remove yourself from it."

"I don't intend to remove myself from it, even if I'm not one of the major players." He turned to Fiona. "But we do need to discuss what's happening. Are you free for dinner tonight?"

She frowned. "Tonight, no, but I don't have anything tomorrow evening."

Murphy gave a little smile. "Fine, where can we meet?"

She smiled. "Here at eight?"

"Good." He nodded at them. "Ladies."

Murphy took the elevator back to his room. *Fiona sounded like she's taking everything in stride, but how did I ever have the nerve to make a date with her? Now I've got to see it through!*

&

Since he was still free that evening Murphy arranged to meet Richard Ambrose for dinner. He arrived at a café took a seat at a table and looked around the room. The ceiling was supported by round pillars which held electric lights with tan and yellow shades. A much bigger shade of the same colors covered the large fixture hanging in the center of the room. The air was filled with cigarette smoke and the aroma of coffee.

Murphy's fists were rigid on the table when Richard arrived and sat. "You look upset."

Murphy gazed back at him. "Nervous is more like it. I was stupid enough to make a date with Fiona for dinner tomorrow."

"How could that be stupid? You should be dancing with joy that she accepted. That's some woman."

Murphy cast his eyes down. "Yes she is. That's the problem. She could run rings around me. Anyway, my excuse for asking her was to discuss some threats by a British agent."

"What type of threats?"

Murphy explained about Bennett. "To make matters worse I'm being followed by a reporter who's determined to drag my name through the mud."

The waiter came and took orders. "George, If the King of England tried to pressure Fiona, he would back off before she did. Guys like the one you met are no more than uncounted beans to her, and the situation in Ireland is creating a lot of bitterness all around. Some British spokesmen have even claimed the Bolsheviks are behind the Irish home rule movement."

An older man at the next table turned to them and spoke with a Russian accent. "Please excuse, I was not listening, but I heard you say Bolsheviks. Are you at the peace conference?" The jacket to his suit had more buttons than Murphy was accustomed to seeing. They extended so high little space was left for the shirt and tie to show through the double-breasted lapels. The fabric of the suit was heavy and appeared to be of good quality but with some worn spots.

Murphy turned toward him. "We are, but not high enough to be of any importance."

The man touched his chest and gave a slight bow. "I am Count Orlofsky, once a colonel of dragoons in the service of our czar, but that is all gone now. Do you deal with Bolsheviks?"

Murphy shifted his chair. "We don't deal with foreign delegations at all. Those things are for the real diplomats We're paper pushers, but from all appearances no one from

Russia or its former empire will be seated. Not you, not the Soviet Russians, not even the Ukrainians."

"If anyone from Russia were being seated, we should be. Those Soviet people, the Bolsheviks, they say they are in control of Russia since they hold Moscow and Saint Petersburg, but the White Army holds more of Russia's land. When we were in power, we stayed in the war. We kept fighting the Germans. Those Bolsheviks, aah. They make deal with them. Why should they be rewarded for—"

"You czarist pig!" Murphy and Richard twisted their necks to see the short Russian woman who was speaking. "How many thousands more Russian boys would have died but for the peace we made? You, the czar, and all those other aristocrats, to you those boys didn't matter. All you cared was for the czar beat the kaiser. Does anyone believe you were really agonizing over Serbia? And you, Lieutenant Murphy, what do you believe?"

Murphy's eyes widened. "How do you know my name?"

She left without a further word. Murphy placed his napkin on the table. "If she were ever given a seat at the conference, I would hate to hear what the debates would sound like."

Count Orlofsky watched the woman leave then shifted his eyes back to Murphy's table. "Now you see part of the problem. But something else is important. If she knew your name and sat so close to you, it was not a coincidence!"

❧

The next evening, back in his hotel room, Murphy bathed with French soap. He shaved for the second time that day, something he didn't usually do. He combed his hair several times before he was happy with the result. After brushing off the jacket, he put on one of his new suits with a powder blue tie which he tied three times before it came out the way he wanted. *Where should I take Fiona for dinner? I'll ask her what she wants.*

When he arrived in the lobby, Fiona was seated on a sofa by herself. Her dress was pale blue to her ankles and was tied tight at the waist with a dark sash. A plunging neckline revealed a gold cross hanging on a thin chain. Her long gloves came up over her elbows, but the round brim on her hat was much narrower than those of her other hats. Murphy had been on dates before but never with a woman who looked and dressed like this. How foolish was he to ask her to dinner?

He made a slight bow. "Bonsoir, Mademoiselle."

Her hands were wrapped over one knee. "Bonsoir, Monsieur. What do you have in store for me?"

Murphy cleared his throat. "I have a few ideas. What's the name of the restaurant on Rue de Castiglione?"

She slid her hands off her knee. "I don't know. Why don't we go to a café tonight? We can relax with some wine and pick whatever we feel like from the menu and not have to stick to dinner items."

He stammered, "Okay, how about the café on Rue de Rivoli? We can walk there."

"That would be perfect."

As they took their seats at the café Murphy squeezed around a potted palm to get to his. He ordered a bottle of red burgundy. The globe lights from a chandelier enabled them to peruse the menus. Murphy lifted his eyes from his.

"No one can identify this Major Bennett, nor has anyone else seen him. Do you think the British are behind this? Maybe I shouldn't say the British, someone from somewhere in the United Kingdom?"

She plunked her menu on the table. "Think of it this way, George. Do the French have any reason to shoo us away? Do the Italians?" She sat back and straightened her shoulders. "Certainly not you Americans. The Germans would like us to be part of the conference. They think we are more likely to be lenient with them than the others." She rested her forearms on the table. "Who else? The Russians? How far do I need to go? Japan or Indochina? At that point we are engaging in fantasy. Instead of looking to the far corners of the earth, we should look to the one faction that has always been adamantly against our playing any role."

The waiter poured each of them a glass of wine. Murphy smiled at Fiona. "You seem to have thought this through."

She smirked. "Could we share a charcuterie platter and a cheese platter?"

"That sounds good." He motioned the waiter over and placed the order.

When he turned back to Fiona, she asked, "Your life, what was it like before you arrived in Paris? From where do you come? Who else is in your family?"

"I'm from Jersey City, like Congressman Hamill. My father is a judge of the Court of Oyer and Terminer, which is the criminal court in New Jersey. I have a brother and a sister."

The waiter placed the cheese platter in front of them. There were five cheeses and some dried fruit, all on a wooden tray. Fiona used her knife to spread some brie on a crisp wafer. "What did you do before you went into the army?"

"I graduated from college in 1916. I thought of going to law school, so I worked for a title abstract company to get experience verifying chains of title to real estate."

"How did you end up in the army?" She took a bite of her cheese.

Murphy sipped his wine. "I joined the New Jersey National Guard after college and was admitted to the officer training program. In the United States the national guard is like the reserve. In peacetime we do some training but still go about our regular jobs. But that changed when the U.S. entered the war. It surprised a lot of people because Woodrow Wilson had campaigned for re-election in 1916 on the fact he had kept us out of the war."

Fiona faced him. The potted palm didn't leave them much room, and her knees touched his leg. "What happened to you afterwards?"

Murphy slid his wine glass around before answering. "My unit got called up. I was a forward observer in the artillery."

She squeezed his shoulder. "How did you get wounded?"

Their faces were close. "I crawled over the top to direct the artillery fire. The Germans shot artillery back at us, and I didn't have the protection of the trench."

She took her hand away. "But now you're with the peace conference delegation."

"When Congressman Hamill found out I was here, he contacted them and said there was a wounded American officer in Paris who had been a French honor student, and suddenly I had a job. I wish I were up to it."

"How could you not be?"

"Oh, I'm fine at translating invoices. It's the other things. The phony crime wave, getting involved with the Belgian woman. I'm no international sophisticate."

The charcuterie platter arrived, and Murphy refilled their glasses. The cold cut meat was on a round wooden tray accompanied by olives and nuts. Murphy rolled a piece of ham onto a wafer. When he finished it he asked her, "Now how about you? What's your story? You clearly possess all the social graces I lack."

She folded her arms on the table and edged closer to Murphy. "I may as well tell you. You'll likely hear about it anyway. George, I ran away from home when I was fifteen. My mother died three years earlier, and my father fell apart. He drank and drank. Do you see the scar over my right eye?"

He raised his eyes to find it. "Yes."

She sat back. "It's from his ring when he punched me. I did not hate him. I was not even angry with him. He was too far gone to rouse those emotions, but I had to get out of there fast. I ran away to Dublin."

Murphy started to pick up an olive but put it back. "What did you do? How did you get by?"

"George, where can a pretty girl always get a job, when she's desperate and has no place to live?"

"You don't mean—"

"Yes I do, George. I worked in a brothel, and don't act morose about it. It was my refuge. There was nowhere else I could turn, and they were good to me there. It's sad for me to say, but it was safer than my own home. My mother taught me manners and how to behave in social situations, and Madame Yvette had a little training program of her own. We were one of the finest such establishments in Dublin and worked with an elite clientele. I entertained some of the top officials and businessmen visiting from Great Britain and from the continent." She flung her head back. "And slept with some of them too."

Murphy was silent. What was he feeling? Not shock. Jealousy? How could she not just survive what she had been through but grow from it? He lifted his head. "You left there?"

She sighed. "I did, after about a year and a half. I met a man somewhat older than I at the library. His name was Sean McDougal, and we became involved. He was working with Michael Collins for home rule and arranged for me to do the same."

"Leaving a brothel, isn't that hard to do?"

She folded her hands on the table and moved her mouth closer to Murphy's ear. "It can be, but not for someone going to work for the people I was. Madame Yvette was leerier of my new connections than I was of hers. She accepted that there was nothing she could do. Also she didn't want to run the risk of having an Irish Republican spy entertaining her clients and listening to their conversations."

"Then what?"

She dropped her head. "Sean was killed in the Easter Rising."

It took Murphy time to respond. "That's awful."

She took a breath. "It was that. I began drinking too much myself, but Collins came to visit me. By then he was higher in the power structure, with Patrick Pearse and so many others having been shot by firing squads. He wanted me to come back and work for them. When Sean was alive

I was just a girl Friday, doing runaround tasks, but now Collins wanted me to do serious political and diplomatic work. It is amazing how working in a brothel turned out to be such good preparation for this type of career."

Murphy walked her back to the Grand Hôtel. They didn't speak much. *She's amazing, being able to suffer through all she did and ending up a spokesperson for Ireland. Even with my education, I couldn't accomplish what she has.* Before they parted in the lobby she buried her head in his shoulder, then lifted it and looked at him with tears in her eyes. She pulled away abruptly and went to the elevator.

As he began the walk back to his hotel he couldn't get his head clear. What was happening? When he turned onto Rue de la Paix he saw the Column Vendome illuminated ahead of him. Something felt wrong. He looked back. He was being followed. There was someone about a block behind him. He wouldn't have noticed if the streets hadn't been so quiet. Murphy turned and walked back toward him. The man ran away. He was too short to be either the mystery man or Major Bennett. A military intelligence agent wouldn't have run away. Who was he?

❧

The following morning, when Murphy arrived at Hôtel de Crillon, his two coworkers were all over him. Richard was the first to speak. "Okay, tell us about this date."

Murphy mumbled, "Oh, you mean with Fiona."

Stephen threw his hands in the air. "Of course we mean with Fiona. How did it go?"

Murphy shrugged. "Yeah, yeah, good, I guess."

CHAPTER VIII

ON THE CHAMPS-ÉLYSÉES, Fiona strolled along window shopping. Why was she in such a quandary? Why did life keep spinning her around? She was happy before she met George Murphy, no, not really happy, but at least content. Why can't she get him out of her head? He may not even like her. He didn't invite her to lunch. He was told to take her, and the baroness pushed him into the dinner invitation. Most men fall all over her. He may have been happy to be rid of her. At least he knows her real story now. How can a man, so brave in battle, be so shy, especially a handsome one, so strong and fit? She had to stop thinking about him. This was the Champs-Élysées. She loved the French style and was comfortable and, she thought, safe in Paris, at least safer than in Ireland. Danger was not new to her, but love was a rare occurrence. Look at what happened the last time. Was that why her thoughts of George scared her so? Why couldn't she have met him when she still had a life of her own? But had she ever? There was no way she could ever have another serious relationship. Her life was dedicated to Irish freedom, for which cause she would undoubtedly, sooner or later, lose it.

As she stopped to admire a dress in a shop window, she smiled at her reflection in the glass and saw a car slow down near the curb behind her. A man with a guard mustache held something out the window, and the glass in front of her shattered. A pain in her chest knocked her to the sidewalk as the gunshot stunned the busy street.

༄

The next morning Murphy took the Metro from Place de la Concorde to meet Claude at the Sorbonne for breakfast. He'd barely passed through the four massive Ionic columns at the entrance to the school when he spotted Claude, but, before he could greet him, another man charged over and scowled at him. Murphy turned his attention to the new person. "Can I help you?

The man's face was beet red, and he clenched his teeth. "What are you doing here. You should be on your way to the guillotine. Why are you not in jail? How many women will they let you kill first?"

Murphy put his hands on his hips. "I haven't killed anybody."

"Then who did?"

"The police have a photo of the prime suspect in Mademoiselle DuBois's murder."

The man glared back at him. "But what about the other, the Irish one? You were seen meeting with the man who shot her."

Murphy froze. "What are you talking about?"

The man's hands were on his hips. "The Irishwoman who was shot on the Champs-Élysées yesterday, who else."

Claude came running over. "Look at this." He handed Murphy the morning edition of *Paris Aujourd'hui*.

Murphy held his breath and grabbed the journal. There was his own face looking back at him on the front page under the headline "Attack on Second Woman Connected to American Army Officer. "The article went on to state his last girlfriend, a Belgian woman was found stabbed to death in his bed. Now, another woman he had been seeing, this time an Irish one, was shot on the Champs-Élysées. Lieutenant Murphy had been seen meeting with the shooter earlier in the Hôtel Continental bar."

He dropped the paper to his side. "Where is she? How badly is she hurt? I have to see Mr. O'Kelly, now." He ran outside and waived down a taxi without thinking if it was rude to Claude and not worrying at all about the other man.

Murphy told the taxi driver to take him to the Grand Hotel. This was really getting to him. He didn't react this way when Angeline was killed, and they were lovers. He arrived at the hotel and raced inside. He looked around but did not see O'Kelly.

A man approached him. "Lieutenant Murphy, I am Lieutenant Coderre. I work with Inspecteur Trudeau at the Préfecture." The officer was about 40 years old with a stocky build for a Frenchman.

Murphy turned to him. "What happened? Where is she?"

Coderre wasted no time. "Fortunately the bullet did not strike her, but a shard of glass hit her in the chest as well as some smaller pieces that had to be removed. She had stitches. I just brought her here from the hospital."

Murphy took a deep breath. "What… what can I do to help?"

All Mademoiselle McDermott could remember about the gunman was that he had a guard mustache. She was looking at clothes in a shop window and saw only his reflection, and that was through the open window of a car. I've been advised you met with a man who had such a mustache, and who made some threats against Mademoiselle McDermott."

"Yes, that's correct. He called himself Major Bennett, said he was from British MI5, but it's not likely to be true."

Coderre's eyes were fixed. "No, it's not. We know the MI5 people here. He's not one of them."

࿐

Murphy was informed that Fiona was in her room, and that breakfast had been sent up. He took the elevator. Sean O'Kelly was in the room with her. He stood. "I'll leave you two alone to talk."

Fiona stared at Murphy. "You came. I was praying you would."

"I… I raced here once I heard."

"Why, George?"

"I don't even know. It's not something I decided to do. It was like some force took control of me. I just had to come."

She smiled. "Not the most romantic language I ever heard, but I think the thought is there."

He smiled back. "I wish I were more skilled in expressing my feelings to you."

She almost laughed. "I think you've managed it all the same, however clumsily."

He sat. "You don't look any the worse for what happened. How do you manage to stay so calm?"

It took her a while to respond. Her eyes appeared to water a little. "George, I have been waiting for this to happen for three years. It's almost anticlimactic. My assailant's major feat was making a mess of the dress shop."

Murphy was fidgeting. "But you were hurt."

"It was only a shard of glass. I just can't wear low cut dresses for a while." She gave a half-smile.

"Are you really okay?"

She pressed her lips together. "I do feel bad about getting shattered glass all over those pretty clothes!"

❧

A message awaited Murphy at the Hôtel de Crillon Saturday morning. General Harts wanted to see him again. Murphy panted as he entered the general's office. "You wanted to see me, sir?"

"Yes, lieutenant." He gestured at an empty chair. "Even though Miss DuBois has not yet been positively identified, both the French and the Belgians feel she should be returned to Belgium for burial. The French are paying for the body to be transported but will not provide an escort. I would like you to perform that duty for several reasons." He held up a finger. "The first is you're one of the few people who knew her." He held up a second finger. "Also, escorting her body home might help refute the runaway allegations you were involved in her murder." He paused and lowered his hand. "It would not hurt for you to take copies of what pictures we have of both her and our mystery man and ask around if anyone recognizes them."

Murphy's head snapped up. "You want me to investigate?"

Harts rested against the back of the chair and put his hands together. "Our intelligence people are competent enough, but the Belgians might resent their probing into something not within American jurisdiction. You, on the other hand, can point out you have no power to arrest or prosecute anyone and, as a staff member of the peace delegation, you are only trying to prevent this incident from interfering with negotiations."

"Where should I look, sir?"

Harts rocked forward on his chair. "We will place a notice with the funeral arrangements in a few Brussels newspapers with a copy of her picture. I want you to keep track of whoever shows up."

Murphy bent his chest forward. "Yes, sir. When do I leave?"

"In three days. The French military will be sending me your travel documents. I will make sure they get to you."

Murphy walked back to the Hôtel de Crillon. So far France was the only foreign country he had ever visited. Now he was going to Belgium. What would he find when he got there? Whom would he find, or, more likely, who would find him? Who might be waiting there? Whoever it was would know he was coming. Should he bring his service weapon? Would paperwork signed by General Harts carry any weight in Belgium?

ꕤ

Fiona was waiting in the lobby of the Grand Hôtel when Murphy picked her up for dinner. The weather was mild, so they strolled to Place de la Madeleine along Boulevard des Capucines. The sidewalk took them past shops. Above were residential apartments bedecked with gorgeous flower boxes. Trees lined both sides of the street. Murphy placed his hand on the small of Fiona's back to follow her through pedestrians coming in the other direction. "I'm going to be away for a few days."

She turned her eyes toward him. "I will miss you, but what is the reason for a trip now?"

"I've just been told I'm escorting Angeline's body back to Brussels. They want me to do some snooping while I'm there."

Fiona stopped dead in her tracks. "George, please be careful. Those people have already killed at least once. They don't shoot and miss!"

ꕤ

At the train station in Brussels Murphy was met by Inspecteur Principal Leclercq of the Belgian police who accompanied him to the vehicle to which Angeline's body was moved. Leclercq did not shake hands when he introduced himself but told Murphy the body was being taken to the medical examiner's office for further study.

Murphy blurted out, "I'm confused. The French police have already done a full examination."

The inspector looked up from his notes. "Monsieur, it is not for suspects to question police procedure."

Murphy's head jerked. "I was the one who had the police called, and I had just left General Harts's headquarters when the murder took place."

The inspector dropped his notebook to his side. "And I have spoken with the detective in Paris who tells me you are the chief suspect. All they need is a motive. Then they will have you. Why are you really here in Belgium?"

Murphy stood dumbfounded with his hands at his sides. "Because General Harts sent me to escort the body."

"Of a woman you claim you hardly knew? Belgian women who survived what happened here deserve our full attention when something like this occurs."

"So you have identified her, and she was Belgian. What was her true name?"

"Monsieur, remember what I said before?"

Murphy pulled out the photo of the mystery man. "You want to see the real suspect? The victim said she encountered this man here in Brussels during the occupation. Have you ever seen him?" Murphy showed him the picture of the mystery man.

Leclercq studied the photo. "I have never seen that man and I was here for the whole occupation. He was not. Now let us do our job. Where are you staying?"

"The Hôtel Metropole."

"You are not under arrest, but do not leave Belgium before the funeral."

Murphy stood still. *Why is this happening? It's the opposite of what General Harts planned. Have I screwed it up again?*

CHAPTER IX

AFTER CHECKING INTO the Metropole, Murphy walked to a tavern. He was shown to a small table away from the windows, sat on the green leather banquette, ordered a glass of red wine, and read through the menu.

Good thing I didn't bring my service weapon to Belgium. General Harts's paperwork would not work here. At least it's safe in Paris behind the headboard of my bed. Even if the maid pulls the bed out to change the linen, she won't see the weapon since the headboard is fixed to the wall.

When the waiter returned with the wine Murphy ordered fish soup to start followed by Belgian endives with ham. As soon as the waiter brought his soup, a middle-aged woman with dark hair walked up to his table. Her dress was tied at the waist with an elaborate cord and there were flower patterns on her hat.

He lifted his head. "May I help you?"

The woman kept a straight face. "I saw your picture in

the paper. You are Lieutenant Murphy. The Belgian woman's body was found in your apartment."

"Yes, I found it and had the concierge call the police."

The woman nodded. "I know. I understand also the victim claimed she was in Leuven during the massacre and was here later."

"That's correct."

The woman's eyes were big and round. "She was not in either place. I was in both. I saw the picture with the death notice in the newspaper. I do not recognize her at all, and no one knows of an Angeline DuBois in either place."

"The name was probably made up. She went by Françoise at the artist studio where she modeled. The fact you don't recognize the picture is more significant. What is your name?"

Her lips curled up slightly. "Martine."

"Is there a last name?"

She moved closer and lowered her voice. "You don't need to know it."

Murphy looked around the room. "What if someone has to follow up on what you told me?"

"They will have no trouble finding me. I will probably find them first anyway."

He needed to keep her talking. "Can I get you anything to eat or drink?"

"I will have wine and some of the fish soup you are having." She slid onto the leather seat next to him.

Murphy ordered a bottle of wine and another fish soup. "Do you live here in Brussels now?"

She turned toward him. "Yes, I cannot bear to go back to Leuven. What this Angeline told you about what happened there, it cannot begin to catch what the horror was like for those of us who, unlike her, were involved. I am not trying to demean her by saying so. The poor girl suffered and died, but we do need to keep our facts straight if we are to accomplish anything."

The waiter brought another soup, a bottle of wine, and another glass. Murphy poured wine into both glasses and offered one to Martine. "What is it you want to accomplish?"

Martine took the glass, set it on the table, and ran her finger along the rim. "The same thing this Angeline told you she wanted, to enforce the Hague Convention."

Murphy turned and put his elbow on the back of the seat. "You and the Armenians. You should get in touch with them. And how do you know so much about what Angeline told me?"

"As to the Armenians, we are in contact, but they are concerned with violations by the Turks, not the Germans. As far as what Angeline may have said to you, a lot of people have sheep in this pen, more than you know. Information gets out and finds its way to me!"

❧

The funeral was being handled by the Belgian government, but Murphy`s only official contact so far had been Inspecteur Principal Leclercq. As he passed the front desk of the hotel on his way from breakfast, the clerk held out a message for him from a Commissaire Mattel. It requested that Murphy stop by his office that morning. He took a taxi to the police station on Rue du Marché au Charbon. The building was well laid out but not so ornate as the one in Paris. He was shown to the Commissaire`s office.

They shook hands. "Bonjour, Lieutenant Murphy. How was your voyage? Are you settled in your hotel?" He gestured to an empty chair.

Murphy took the seat. "Yes thank you, sir, but may I ask, does your department consider me a suspect in Miss Dubois`s murder?"

Mattel closed the file on his desk. "We do not have suspects because we are not conducting the investigation. The French police are."

"Inspecteur Principal Leclercq seems to think otherwise."

"Please excuse him. He has two sisters who were badly abused during the German occupation. Unfortunately the first account he read of Mademoiselle DuBois's murder was the one written by Henri Durand, who's obviously no friend of yours. Now he has been in contact with the detective in Paris, who seems convinced that you are the killer. It seems unlikely to me. What motive could you have? Also, people who do that type of thing usually have a trail of incidents. You have none. This thing with the Irishwoman doesn't fit either. Thrill killers don't hire other people to do the job."

Murphy breathed a sigh. *I'm not a screwup. I might accomplish what I came here to do?* "Thank you. It makes things easier. What is being done about Mademoiselle DuBois's funeral?"

Mattel put the closed file on the table behind him. "The pastor of the Church of St. Mary Magdalene is conducting a funeral Mass in two days at eleven o'clock in the morning. A notice will be placed in the paper. There will be many eyes looking at whoever comes. It will be a blessing if someone shows up who does know who she is. Have you learned anything since you arrived here?"

"I met a woman at dinner last night. She said she was from Leuven and that Mademoiselle DuBois was not, and she said her name was Martine but would not give a last name."

Mattel gave what passed for a smile. "That would be Martine Joossens. She may act mysterious, but pay her good attention. She has sources of information developed clandestinely during the occupation, sources even we can't access. In the past she has been known to take matters into her own hands. She will never tell you what she has up her sleeve until she needs you to know. Asking her questions is a waste of time. If she has the information you need, she will decide when and where to make it known to you. If she does choose to tell you something, take it seriously, but tell me, are you doing some type of investigation?"

Murphy recalled the official line. "I'm solely a liaison whose purpose is to keep these events from interfering with the goals of the peace conference."

The commissaire's eyebrows rose. "How could that happen?"

Murphy collected himself. "Our concern is with a pattern of events starting with a series of newspaper articles falsely alleging a crime wave by American soldiers. We have Mademoiselle DuBois's murder and threats against the woman in the unrecognized Irish delegation. I'm not acting in any law enforcement capacity, but solely from a diplomatic one. I have no authority to bring charges against anyone anywhere."

Mattel reclined against the back of the chair. "I can

appreciate your concern, but you need to realize what you are dealing with here in Belgium. You have been in France some months, but it is not the same thing. France was an active belligerent in the war. We were neutral, but were invaded anyway."

"Isn't that what brought Britain into the war?"

Mattel`s eyelids drooped. "Not only were we occupied, but the occupation began with great brutality and abuse by a country we had neither declared war against nor attacked. In addition to raping our women, killing both men and women and destroying valuable artifacts, they carried off thousands of our men to labor camps in Germany."

"Have the men taken to the labor camps all been returned?"

Mattel raised his eyes. "Some have. It's still too early to tell how many were or will be. Admittedly the French suffered great losses on the battlefield, both of human life and to their countryside, but facing such horrors in battle is not the same as facing them in your own backyard. That is why even the slightest suggestion Mademoiselle DuBois was a Belgian victim of those events elicits enormous concern. I tell you this so you will keep in mind any person you interview is probably nurturing a wound of his own, and his response will be colored by it."

Murphy stood. "Will the fact I am an American be a factor?"

"It will help. Your Herbert Hoover helped prevent starvation here during the first years of the war. The Germans had no objection to a neutral country shipping us food. But once you entered the war, that was no longer permitted. Now Hoover is trying to do the same thing for the starving Germans, and the British are stopping him despite the armistice."

⁂

That evening Murphy found himself dining with Claude at an establishment called *Friture Léon* on Rue des Bouchers.

They were shown to a table with a green checkered cloth. Murphy pulled out a chair and slid behind the table against a golden wood paneled wall. "Can you tell me now what you're doing here in Brussels?"

Claude pulled out a low armchair and took a seat. "I didn't want to say this at the reception desk at the hotel, but my father asked me to come. There may be information here that will help with the murder investigation. It is a matter for the French authorities, but, as you have seen, not everyone in Belgium sees it that way. My presence will draw less suspicion, as I knew her, and also know you."

"Given no one here knows who Angeline was, do you think she was from Belgium at all?" The waiter came to take their order.

Claude ordered beer and mussels for both of them. "George, I am a Frenchman. I know how Belgians talk, not like us French. Believe me this lady spoke French with a Belgian accent an actress could not imitate, even with training. Also, actresses have a script and can memorize specific lines in an accent other than their own. Angeline had no way of knowing what might be said in any conversation. Her Belgian accent was real."

"But how come nobody remembers her?"

The waiter placed two glasses of Belgian beer on the

table. Claude took a sip of his. "Mon ami, I do not know, but what about this new girlfriend of yours, the Irish one? Why is she being targeted?"

Murphy plunked his glass on the table. "My girlfriend__ Fiona? I guess you could call her that. I don't know what else to call her. We went from icy to close so quickly. More quickly than could have happened in any other setting. How often does a woman you've just taken to lunch get shot at and wounded?"

"Bizarre." Claude sat back to allow the waiter to place two cast iron pots full of steaming mussels on the table. The aroma of onions settled around them.

"That's the only word that can describe it." Murphy dropped his head. "She's an extremely complex woman who's had a difficult life. The first time we met she acted like she would rather have a tooth pulled than go to lunch with me. Later she became charming. Then the roof fell in, and we were thrust together. Before all that happened I had about as much chance of making her my girlfriend as I did of being promoted to general."

Claude spooned mussels from the pot into his bowl. "But you seem to be captivated by her. You were not like this with Angeline. There is a reason for this, maybe?" He used his fork to pry a mussel from its shell.

"I can't say what Angeline was. Hell, I don't even know *who* she was. Fiona sometimes seems like she's removed from reality. She lives in her own world but knows how to control the real world around her. I don't know if I'm capable of keeping up with her. She's a highly sophisticated woman who's seen a lot in her short life. I feel like a country bumpkin by comparison."

"But, unlike eighty percent of your army, you're not from the country. You're a college graduate, an army officer and a decorated veteran, not a donkey cart driver."

Murphy turned his eyes away. "There are times when I feel so lacking in poise I may as well be sitting behind a donkey."

"Does she treat you like she feels that way?"

"No, not at all. As a matter of fact she's told me a lot of personal things I was surprised she shared." Murphy began working on the mussels.

"George, something is happening to you."

George looked up from his bowl. "As to your question, I doubt the British government is behind the threats to Fiona, but that doesn't rule out private groups opposed to home rule for Ireland, organizations which I know nothing about. Why do I always find myself in this situation? Why am I so ineffective? Is it because I am so inexperienced?"

"George, the false reports started over a year and a half ago." He pushed his beer glass aside. "Neither the French police nor the entire allied intelligence community have been able to pin down the source. How does the fact you have not been able to solve all of this in a few days make you, what word did you use, ineffective?"

That evening Fiona dined at Maxim's. She wore a black broad-brimmed hat and a tight full-length rust colored dress. Her companion, a thin man in his fifties, sported an elegant gray suit. He had approached her in the afternoon in the Grand Hôtel lobby, identified himself as Herr

Ostomeyer, a member of the unseated German delegation, and invited her to join him for dinner. At the restaurant he did not consult her before ordering a bottle of fine Bordeaux. "We can be of much use to each other."

She interlocked her fingers on the table. "Pray tell."

"The English don't want either of us here, and they will succeed in keeping us both from having any say about the treaty, but it won't stop there." He tapped the table with his finger. "Everyone knows the treaty will be unenforceable, even the big four. They want to appease their electorates. But what will happen after? That is where we come in. Germany will pretend to give in, but in the end we will not. All we are doing is buying time. What we will need is someone to take us out of this, a real leader."

Fiona rolled her eyes. "What do I have to do with this?"

He half smiled. "Do you think the English are going to let you have what you want, a government of your own?"

She pulled her hands apart. "What they will let us have and what we will have are not the same thing."

Ostomeyer spread his lips into something that almost looked like a broad smile. "Exactly, and, when Germany is back on its feet, we can help make what you want happen."

Her eyes were just visible under the brim of her hat. "In exchange for what?"

The sommelier arrived with the wine and, after Ostomeyer tasted it, poured two glasses. "Neither side is in a position yet to make offers of anything. All we can do now is to establish a friendly relationship."

She looked away from him, studied an elaborate mirror in front of a mural, and sipped her wine. "Herr Ostomeyer, we are open to talking with anyone, but we have no ability to enter into treaties or alliances, and were we to get too close to you, we would alienate some of our own base. The Irish lost a lot of soldiers in this war too."

"Yes, fighting for the British at the same time the British were shelling the Dublin Post Office." He drank some wine.

"Some feel that way. Some do not." She took a larger swig from her glass.

Ostomeyer pointed his finger at her. "Think of it this way. There will be another war, and next time we will win. We won't be lulled into marching off the field, undefeated, only to be told the fourteen points both sides agreed to as the basis of the armistice will not be honored. We will fight until it is over. Don't you want to be on the winning side? At that point you will not have to go begging to the British hat in hand. You will be able to dictate to them."

Fiona dropped her eyes and concentrated on her wine.

After they finished their dinner, Fiona declined an Armagnac, and Ostomeyer sent for his car. As they drove off, the driver made a right turn on Avenue Gabriel, the opposite direction of the Grand Hôtel.

Fiona glanced out the window. "Where are we going? This is not the way back to my hotel."

Ostomeyer slid up against her and placed his hand on her knee. "The night is still young, Fiona. Let's have some fun."

She snuggled up against him and whispered in his ear. "We could do that back at my hotel."

Ostomeyer laughed. "So you can disappear into your delegation? I don't think so, Fiona." He grabbed her shoulders and pressed his mouth against hers while he pulled down the front of her dress.

Fiona didn't hesitate. She reached up to her head, whipped out her hatpin, and plunged it into the base of his neck. As he screamed, the car screeched to a stop, and Fiona scrambled out the door.

CHAPTER X

MURPHY AND CLAUDE took the train to Leuven the next morning and walked to the ruins of the Catholic University Library. For a while they stood with their mouths open. The floors were all gone, and there was nothing but rubble inside. Only a handful of walls remained.

Murphy shook his head, "Although it was unlimited submarine warfare that ultimately brought the United States into the war, there were three events which took us to the edge before: the sinking of the Lusitania, the execution of British nurse Edith Cavell and the burning of this library. Why did the Germans do it? It served no military purpose. In 1914 they claimed they were only defending themselves from Belgian resisters. What did they think the Belgians were going to do, throw books at them?"

Claude spun around. "Let's go. I need a drink."

Murphy followed him. "I'm with you."

They found a nearby local café and ordered two cognacs. A Belgian man walked up to them, his eyes on

Murphy. "You're Lieutenant Murphy. I saw your picture in the newspaper."

Murphy stood and offered his hand. "Do you live here in Leuven?"

The man took his hand. "I do, but your friend Miss DuBois did not. She has been the principal subject of conversation at every café in Leuven for several days now."

Murphy nodded. "We are here for the funeral. It may be our last chance to see if anyone knows who she is."

The man's eyes widened. "Don't hold your breath!"

Fiona was at the Préfecture de Police listening to Lieutenant Coderre. "We have already checked with the German delegation. They do not have anyone named Ostomeyer in their party, nor was the car you rode in last night one of theirs. Its license plate was fake. None of the staff at Maxim's recognized the man, although they all recognized you. Why did this person want to meet with you?"

"He claimed it was to get Ireland to support Germany in the next war, which he assured me was coming."

Coderre stiffened. "Seriously, mademoiselle?"

She folded her hands. "That's what he said, but if it was what he wanted, he would never have attacked me afterwards."

"Might assaulting you have been his real purpose?"

She edged forward. "Were it so, he would have skipped going to Maxim's altogether, where he would be seen in my company by many people. We went there in his car. Whatever he was planning, he wanted to make a show of it."

"Might I suggest, before going off with anyone you don't already know, you verify they are who they say they are." He presented a card to her. "Please take this in case you need to call me. Maybe it's someone whose only purpose is to scare and upset you, but we can't be sure."

ର

Friday morning Murphy and Claude took a taxi to the Church of St. Mary Magdalene on Rue de la Magdeleine. The church was small but impressive, dating from the thirteenth century. Particularly grand were the five stained glass windows above the sanctuary depicting the redemption. They were greeted by none other than Inspecteur Principal Leclercq who was somewhat civil. Murphy introduced Claude to him, and Leclercq introduced both Murphy and Claude to the pastor who was to celebrate the Mass.

The priest extended his hand. "Welcome to St. Mary Magdalene, gentlemen. I trust you did not have too much trouble getting here."

Murphy took his hand. "We did not. Thank you, father." Murphy scanned the ceiling. "This is a magnificent church. I do admire the windows."

"If you look at the bottom left of the third window on the side, you will see depicted the martyr St. Nicholas Pieck, who preached in this church in the sixteenth century. But I understand you are more interested in seeing who attends this service. Alors, I will not hold you." He left them.

Leclercq turned to Murphy. "I've notified the railroad that you are not allowed to leave the country."

Murphy stiffened. "What?"

He had a half-smile. "I need to take a detailed statement about what happened at your apartment. Be at my office tomorrow at four in the afternoon."

"What do you mean?"

"Be there." Leclercq proceeded to the vestibule of the church.

Murphy and Claude sat on the far right side of the church, so they could turn and see who came and went. Leclercq stood near the entrance. As it got closer to eleven o'clock, the church filled up. No one sat in the front of the church other than Martine, whose last name Murphy now knew was Joossens. All the rest sat as far back as possible. At eleven o'clock the coffin was carried in and the service began. At the conclusion, it was carried out as the organ played.

Murphy turned as the coffin passed. *Who's that standing in the vestibule? He's staring at me. Those narrow eyes and straight lips, they're the ones that scared Angeline away. It's the mystery man, the same one as in the photograph.*

Murphy raced toward the back, but, no matter how many times he said "Pardon" or "Excusez-moi," all he got back from the crowd were blank stares. Leclercq saw him coming, looked around, spotted the mystery man and recognized him from the photograph. He grabbed the man who then pulled a pocketknife and slashed the inspecteur's arm. He drew the knife back to lunge with it, but spotted Murphy coming at him, only ten feet away, and ran out the door instead. Murphy whipped off his jacket, rolled it up and used it to stem Leclercq's bleeding. An ambulance was called. Before he got on Leclercq thanked Murphy and cancelled the interview for the next day.

⁂

The following morning, in Paris, Fiona slept late and went for breakfast in the Grand Hôtel. The other delegates had already finished, so she sat by herself in a comfortable red leather chair beneath an Ionic column where she had tea and pastry.

As she drank her tea, a man approached her. "Miss McDermott, I'm Captain Sanders from MI5. May I sit and have a word with you?"

She looked him over. He was about thirty years old, slim, and clean-shaven. His suit was well tailored. "Where is your guard mustache?"

He smirked. "I've never had one, but I assure you I am from MI5, unlike the so-called Major Bennett."

"You may sit if you mean to tell me why you want to talk to me."

He took the chair opposite her. "Thank you, but your question about the guard mustache indicates you already know the reason. Let me assure you I have no interest in interfering with your work here. While our delegation might be opposed to your presence, I'm not a politician, and I'm not a diplomat."

She forced a smile. "What are you then?"

Sanders let out his breath. "Being in counterintelligence is like being a constable on patrol. Our job is to prevent trouble, and someone attacking you is trouble, especially when he pretends to be one of us. It's not just a problem for you, but for us as well. If anyone were to harm you here, it would damage our relationships with both France and the United States, relationships that are enormously critical to us right now."

"And to us."

"I want to make it clear we have no idea who this Major Bennett is. The only ones we know who have seen him are you and your friend Lieutenant Murphy."

She sipped her tea. "You did not come here just to tell me that."

He used a softer voice. "I understand, Miss McDermott, but your safety is still at risk. Even though you might resent the thought, our government still regards you as a British subject. I don't say that to try to restrict your activity, but only to make you aware that we can extend our protective ring to you, which we could not do, if you were regarded as a foreigner. You would be safer if we could share information with each other about the threats to your person."

"How? How is that the case? No one is going to provide me with a bodyguard, nor is there the likelihood of any arrests forthcoming. Why would belonging to some type of coalition along with people who, by your own admission, do not want me here in the first place, make me any safer?" A white coated waiter came and topped off her cup. "Even if I did have information you are looking for, I cannot see myself sharing it with your government. Please, this is not personal. You may be sincere in everything you say, but our experiences with others in your government have taught us to be wary." She picked the pastry back up and took a bite.

"Anyway, at least you know we are willing to help if you have any need." He handed her a card. "This has our telephone number at the Majestic Hôtel if you wish to contact us."

She put it in her purse as he left. Who is good and who

is evil in this whole mess? Captain Sanders was probably a decent man, truly concerned with preventing violence to anyone including her. But even if his superiors didn't want her harmed, they didn't want her to succeed either.

Fiona left the dining room. *My one goal in my life is a free Ireland. As a little girl I dreamed of being married to a man with a prosperous farm and having children, but that was before becoming disreputable. Not a handicap in my current situation. It taught me how to be a good diplomat, but it didn't do much for my hope of being a respectable matron of a family farm. What about George? Our relationship has gone too far to ignore, but where can it go from here? My past didn't turn him off, but a bullet would make that irrelevant. There's work to be done which must take the place of all my other desires. So, I'll use my charms the same as I did with my clients at Madame Yvette's—including with this new Captain Sanders.*

CHAPTER XI

MURPHY SPENT THE rest of the day going over the incident with the commissaire. Saturday he took a late train back to Paris. When he arrived at Gare de Nord railway station, a car pulled up. The driver got out and spoke with a German accent. "Lieutenant Murphy, I am a driver with the German delegation. Major Muller would like to meet with you at your hotel to discuss the incident involving Miss McDermott at Maxim's as soon as possible. He sent me to bring you."

"Incident, Maxim's, what are you talking about?"

The man shrugged his shoulders. "She was not harmed, but the major wanted to talk about it."

Murphy got in and was driven to the main entrance of the Hôtel Continental on Rue de Castiglione. He got out, thanked the driver and walked to the door, where he heard someone say, "Good evening, lieutenant." It was the reporter, Henri Durand.

Murphy went inside. Muller wasn't anywhere. When

Murphy asked for him at the desk, he was told they had not seen him. Murphy told the desk clerk, if Muller arrived, he would be in his room. He heard nothing further, called the Grand Hôtel but couldn't reach Fiona. *What happened with Fiona? Why would Muller send a car to bring me here and then disappear himself?*

ೞ

Late Sunday morning Fiona went to Mass at Sainte Chapelle on Île de la Cite, the same island in the Seine as Notre Dame Cathedral. It was smaller and was completed earlier. She found a seat in the large upper chapel with high stained glass windows and a vaulted ceiling. She delighted in watching the differing rays of light created by the tinted glass. When the Mass ended she got up to leave along with a press of other people. As the crowd pushed toward the exit, she bumped into a man. When she turned to apologize, she spotted George behind him. She had not seen him since he left for Brussels. Once they got outside, he gently took her arm. "I tried to reach you last night. I heard you had some type of incident at Maxim's."

Her shoulders stiffened. "You could call it 'some type of incident' alright." She told him what had happened.

He looked back at her. "Wow, remind me never to offend you."

"George, that would never happen. Please, it was a serious attack that could have ended up a lot worse."

"I'm sorry. You're right. It was my clumsy way of admiring your fortitude."

She shifted her eyes at him. "I already knew that. I just wanted to make sure *you* realized it."

Murphy filled Fiona in on what had happened in Belgium, and she told him about her encounter with Captain Sanders.

Murphy grimaced. "Can I take you over to Île Saint-Louis for something to eat?"

She smiled back at him.

Looking toward Île Saint-Louis, from the bridge, they could see red awnings wrapped around the outside of a five story building. As they got closer, they found it was a tavern called *L'Oasis*. There were iron railings at every level. The first floor had green vines overhanging the awning. After inspecting the chalkboard menu at the entrance they decided to give it a go. Almost an hour later they came out well satisfied with their choice.

Murphy put his hand on Fiona's shoulder. "Getting back to Maxim's, what could this Ostomeyer person's purpose have been? Even if we don't accept the German delegation's denials, if he was looking for Irish support for a German cause, it would make no sense for him to assault you afterwards. If assault was his real purpose, why would he choose such an elaborate setting?"

She raised her eyes to his. "You left out one possibility, that he was working for northern Irish militia, and this was related to Bennett's threat, disguised to look like it was coming from a different country."

Murphy took her hand. "Are you going back to your hotel from here?"

Her eyes were wide. "I am."

He straightened up. "Let me walk you there. I'm no

security guard, but the less you're alone on public streets, the better."

"You don't need an excuse to escort me, George."

They didn't talk much on the way as they were busy negotiating the traffic. In addition to automobiles and pedestrians there were horse drawn wagons and buggies, not grand coaches with teams of horses, but small Hansom cabs with the driver in the back and the reins running over the roof.

Fiona slid her hand into his. *Wake up, Fiona, you haven't been a schoolgirl in a long time. Can I handle this relationship now, with everything that's happening?*

ꟹ

When Murphy arrived back in the lobby at the Hôtel Continental and found Major Muller waiting for him, he demanded, "What happened to you last night?"

Muller squinted at Murphy. "Last night? What are you talking about?"

"Your driver picked me up at Gare de Nord. He said he was bringing me here where you would meet me. I arrived, and you were nowhere to be found."

Muller's chin dropped to his chest. "I have no driver. I have no car, but what you are saying might explain this." He put a copy of the day's newspaper on the table. It recounted the incident at Maxim's involving Fiona and Ostomeyer but also stated Lieutenant Murphy, already suspected of being behind an earlier attack, was seen Saturday evening getting out of a car at his hotel. The car appeared to be the one in which Mademoiselle McDermott was assaulted. It even had the same fake license plate number.

Murphy threw the paper on the table. "And of course that damn reporter, Durand, was at the door."

Muller took the paper back and rolled it up. "So now we know the reason for this whole Ostomeyer show. It was another charade to implicate you in Miss McDermott's troubles. The reason I wanted to talk to you lieutenant is we both need to resolve this situation."

Murphy spread his hands. "My ability to help is somewhat limited. The French police are in charge. I am merely a liaison."

Muller's chest puffed up. "No, I am sorry, but you are more than that. You were with Miss DuBois when the mystery man frightened her. He was following you when he was photographed. Miss DuBois was murdered in your apartment. You found her body. In addition, you now appear to be Miss McDermott's closest companion. Now she is a victim, and certain elements of the press are targeting you."

Well I may as well tell you. I saw the mystery man again in Brussels at Angeline Dubois's funeral. He was back in the vestibule of the church. I couldn't reach him, but a Belgian police official did, only to get slashed with a knife. The man raced away before I could get to him, and I had to deal with the wounded detective."

Muller's eyebrows shot up. "The mystery man was in Brussels at Miss DuBois's funeral! That… Is your English expression, 'throws a new light?'"

Murphy's eyes widened. "How is that?

Muller gazed up. "He was obviously involved in Miss DuBois's murder, but she is dead now. Still he follows you to Belgium, so, whatever his purpose, it is ongoing."

Murphy shrugged his shoulders. "That much we already know."

Muller waved his hand. "Hear me. No matter what anyone has told you, the mystery man is not German. If he were, I would know it by now. But, whoever he is, it is clear that he is targeting you. This ploy with the car from the railroad station suggests as much."

Murphy shook his head. "Of what possible interest could I be to them?"

"On your own, none. But they obviously see you as the path to whomever or whatever their real target is."

~

Murphy met with Commissaire Trudeau that afternoon. He did not have to wait long to be shown into the office. After greetings were exchanged Trudeau said, "You can't seem to get away from adventure no matter where you go, lieutenant."

Murphy replied, "I don't think it is so much that adventure follows me as that one particular person does."

"That is a good point, lieutenant."

"Where do we go from here?"

"This is not just an unsolved murder. We have to consider it as one link in an ongoing conspiracy. In addition to the DuBois murder we have two attacks on Mademoiselle McDermott. In most ways they appear to be unrelated with the one exception that both women had some connection to you. That can be both good and bad. Good in that, if we can find out who is following you and why, we may solve both situations. Bad in that other crimes may still be committed."

"What do you want to do?"

"It might be advisable to conduct counter surveillance of you in case you are still being followed. I know your own MID was doing that, but I suspect their limited personnel are all recognizable at this point. I would like to use my own people. I can pull a wider range of officers, less likely to be recognized. In order to do this it will be necessary to coordinate it with your military governor, General Harts."

"You're right about the MID tail becoming too easy to identify. On one occasion, not only did I spot him, but a German major did as well!"

ᘛ

Thursday evening, as Murphy returned from work and walked toward the elevator, he encountered Sean O'Kelly. "Lieutenant Murphy, I just visited Congressman Hamill. Do you have a moment to sit and talk?"

"Yes of course."

O'Kelly took an armchair in the lobby, and Murphy sat on a couch to his right facing a cocktail table. *What is this leading to?*

O'Kelly clasped his hands and rested them against his chest. "Fiona has been notified her father has died."

Murphy stiffened. What should he say? He mumbled, "Oh, how will it affect her? I don't believe they were close."

O'Kelly's speech was soft. "Even being estranged it is having an emotional impact on her. It will also have a financial impact."

Murphy fidgeted. "How? He certainly wasn't doing anything to support her."

O'Kelly had an easy smile. "No, he wasn't, but he will."

"You're probably tired of my asking how."

O'Kelly's manner was gentle. "He never took her out of his will. She's his sole heir. Despite his drunkenness the farm always turned a good profit. He employed fourteen full-time field hands who kept it running. It's a big farm, with no liens against it. Fiona owns it outright now."

For almost half a minute Murphy just stared at the framed pictures on the wood paneled wall. *After all the abuse and scorn she endured she's now an heiress.* He lowered his gaze. "What does she plan on doing?"

O'Kelly sat up straight. "She refuses to give up her work at the conference but will go back for the funeral. She also has to take care of business, assure the hands their jobs are safe, change the bank accounts into her name and all."

Murphy fumbled with his hands. "I will have to speak to her."

O'Kelly removed his eyeglasses. "You can do more than that now! Can't you?"

Murphy tensed up. "What do you have in mind?"

O'Kelly stared him right in the eye. "Go to Ireland with her. She needs you. The situation there is precarious, and she would be much safer with you by her side."

Murphy drew his breath in. *If I go with her, it won't stop there. I will have to see this whole thing through to the finish, and Bennett, whoever he really is, becomes my scourge. But isn't he already, even if I'm not the one he shot at? If I don't go with her now, there will be no tomorrow, not with Fiona. I can't bear that thought. Will they let me leave Paris? Will it cost me my job and all the other things I wanted to do in Paris?* He swallowed. *It doesn't matter.* "When are we going?"

"In three days. You can travel on Sunday, and Fiona will be there Monday morning to take care of business. It will also give you time to talk to Ambassador White."

CHAPTER XII

WHITE LOOKED ACROSS his ornate desk at Murphy. "Lieutenant, I won't insult you by explaining how volatile the situation is now in Ireland. I'm sure Miss McDermott's firsthand experience enables her to do so more effectively, at least from her perspective. Nothing has been the same there since the Easter Rising three years ago. While it was a military victory for the British, it was a political disaster for them you must stay clear of. But you're right about one thing. If you don't go with her the French press will continue to come down on you like a ton of bricks, not just about the attack on Miss McDermott, but about the DuBois murder as well. That would hurt the conference more than your absence for a few days. But remember, you are going there to escort a friend to her father's funeral, nothing else. Things are too unsettled here to have any friction with the British delegation."

"I do understand, sir." *Where is this leading?* Murphy sat still.

The ambassador's droopy white mustache moved as he spoke. "At the conference we prefer you to wear civilian clothes as you go about your duties, but for this trip to Ireland I think it best if you go in uniform. The situation is tense, and there are elements on both sides who can be a little overaggressive. They are apt to be more cautious of a uniformed American officer than they would be of some unknown man escorting Miss McDermott."

When Murphy got back to his office, he was stunned to see Fiona standing there at his desk. Her left arm was bent so that the tips of her fingers touched her throat. He placed his hands on her shoulders. "Fiona, I'm so sorry to hear about your father. I know there were problems, but it must still come as a shock."

Her voice was barely a whisper. "It does that George. It makes me think of what he was like before my mother died. It is what I missed even more than I realized. I was so scared. It kept me from trying to find out how he was doing."

Murphy could feel a slight tremor in her body. He pulled her closer and kissed her on the forehead.

Her eyes were moist, if not yet teary. "George, this is the first time you've ever kissed me."

"I didn't plan it that way. It just happened."

She finally managed a smile. "Does that mean I should wait for a kiss that has been thought through in more detail?"

"No, I don't know what I mean."

She stared at her feet before speaking. "I understand you're taking me back to Ireland for the funeral."

"Yes, and I've been authorized to go as long as I wear my uniform. Ambassador White wants everyone conscious of the fact I'm an American army officer. He feels both sides will be less likely to make trouble."

She flashed a full smile at this. "That's not just a good idea. It's a wonderful one. Everybody there is looking for American support." She chirped. "I'll be busy getting ready today. Can we meet tonight?"

"Yes, I'll pick you up for dinner. How's seven-thirty? By the way, how did you get here today?

"Seven-thirty is good, and one of our security people brought me here. You needn't worry."

෴

Fiona was waiting on a couch in the lobby when Murphy arrived at the Grand Hôtel. She rubbed the top of his hand with hers. "Where are you taking me?"

"How about *Capucines?*"

"Oh, that's delightful!"

When they arrived they were shown to a table for two on the second floor in a window alcove overlooking the boulevard. The room was adorned in various shades of the color red. It was bright on the lampshades and cushions, dark on the molding and woodwork, and scarlet on the oriental rugs and glass ceiling. Murphy ordered a bottle of Côtes du Rhone. After it was poured he lifted his glass. "Would it be appropriate to drink to your father?"

"Someone should, and who better than us." She held up her own glass. "To Daa!"

"To your daa!"

When the waiter came back Murphy ordered escargots to start followed by calf's liver persillé for himself and onion soup followed by Salmon d'Ecosse for Fiona. He turned back toward her. "What should we expect tomorrow?"

Fiona slid her glass around. "In addition to my official chores I will have to cope with the neighbors who I am sure have heard the worst about me."

It took him a moment. "How bad do you think it will be?"

Her eyes shifted around the room and back. "Not as bad as it would be if I did not now employ people there and supply local merchants with business. No one will say anything to my face, but there will be a lot of covert whispering, whispering that is sure to include speculation about you. I am not looking forward to having to make arrangements for the funeral with the parish priest."

"Will it be that bad?"

She pressed her lips together before speaking. "I don't know, but my spicy past is not going to be our biggest problem. It might make for a lot of gossip, but, in Ireland today, people are much more concerned with not getting killed than they are with sex scandals. Many are committed to one side or the other, but there are an awful lot of people who would just like to sit it out and then cozy up to the winner."

"Where will we stay?"

Fiona puffed up. "That's one thing we don't have to worry about. The farmhouse, my farmhouse will be right comfortable. My father employed a housekeeper. It was always well kept. There will be plenty of food in. You don't have to worry. You will be *my* guest."

"So we do have a safe haven there."

She lowered her eyes and took a deep breath. "I hope so, George. This was the home where I grew up. For the first twelve years of my life it was my castle, my fortress, my garden, my secret enclave. But then it became my hell. How am I going to react when I walk back in there? I am afraid of myself."

Murphy glanced at the ceiling. *She's coming out of her shell, finally.* "I think that's the real reason Mr. O'Kelly wanted me to go with you."

She tightened her lips into a forced smile. "It is certainly one. That it is."

When they finished eating they walked back to the hotel along Boulevard des Capucines. There was no way of walking on the street with Fiona without being noticed. She wore a long beige dress that was tight at the waist but flared out at the bottom. The jacket was the same color and also form fitting. It was fastened below the throat and came to the level of her knees. Her hat was a darker shade of beige and had a broad round brim. Murphy took her left arm. She reached her right arm around and squeezed his. Without a word she withdrew her left arm, threw it around Murphy's neck and pressed her lips against his. Murphy used his free right arm to grab her around the waist and pull her toward him. They finally broke apart. "I guess you enjoyed the dinner a lot!"

"Oh, George, I wanted to make sure that all I got was not another peck on the forehead. You didn't have time to plan this one either!"

ᔕ

Murphy had a car and driver from the American delegation motor pool take him to the Grand Hôtel to pick up Fiona. She arrived in the lobby wearing a long dark skirt and an embroidered white blouse with long sleeves. There was a blue ribbon tied with a bow at her throat, and her hat, while round, was not at all broad. Instead of high heels she wore long boots. She was respectable, but not the usual elegant Fiona. Her eyes were fixed on him. "I have never seen you in your uniform before. It's quite smart. What are those ribbons?"

Murphy pointed. "One is a Sliver Star, and another is a Purple Heart. Which means I got wounded."

She ran the tips of her fingers over them. "It will be hard for me to keep the ladies away from you."

He snickered. "I don't think you'll have any trouble!"

They were driven to the Saint-Lazare Station where they boarded the train for Cherbourg. From there they took the ferry to Ireland. It was a choppy ride. The only ferries Murphy had ever taken before went across the Hudson River. Those boats did not have to contend with rising and falling over great swells. This one did.

In Dublin the customs agent took one look at Murphy in his American uniform and quickly stamped their passports without asking any questions.

As they left the terminal Fiona pranced along. "That is the easiest I have ever gotten through here. Your uniform does wonders."

Murphy shifted his eyes in her direction. "I thought it was my charming personality."

Her eyes met his. "Is that what you call sarcasm?"

He shrugged. "No, no, I'll remember to thank the ambassador."

She smirked back at him.

It was already dark outside. They were approached by

a middle-aged man wearing a suit and tie, trench coat and hat. He touched the brim of his hat. "Mr. Collins sent us to collect you. Our car is over there in the lot."

When they got to the vehicle there was another man, younger, in the driver's seat. He was dressed the same as the other. The car was large enough for the four of them, with Murphy and Fiona in the back. The roof was made of canvas and could be opened. Their escorts neither introduced themselves nor asked Fiona and Murphy's names.

"To Dungarvan, it will be about four hours." The man put Fiona's valise in the boot and let Murphy do his own before they set off.

They started out through the harbor area with storage tanks, trucks and scrapyards. They came to a commercial area and crossed the River Liffey on O'Connell Bridge. It was Murphy's first time in Ireland, and this was one of the finest parts of Dublin. As they passed Trinity College, Murphy looked up at the grand stone columns and the Roman arched doorway. The railings on the windows were also made of stone. Finally they made it out of Dublin and into the countryside. Without the city lights it was too dark to see anything.

At the outskirts of Waterford, a police car was parked at the side of the road in front of them. An officer got out and held up his hand for them to stop.

Their older escort smacked his hand on his thigh. "Ah, now we're in for it!"

The officer held a square flashlight with a lantern handle on the top. He pointed it at the back seat and at Murphy. "Ahhh, what have we here? Is this the new uniform of the IRA? What are you, a bloody general?"

Murphy rolled his eyes. "It's First Lieutenant, United States Army."

The officer froze and mumbled, "You may pass."

As they drove off, Fiona gazed out the window. "Aren't you glad now you wore your uniform?"

The older escort grinned. "That fixed him. It's the easiest we've ever gotten through a roadblock!"

CHAPTER XIII

IT WAS WELL past the dinner hour when they arrived at the farmhouse, but Mrs. Fitzpatrick, the housekeeper, had kept food hot for them. When Fiona walked in the door, Mrs. Fitzpatrick embraced her with tears in her eyes before holding her at arm's length. "Oh Fiona, it's been so long, but look at you. You're all grown-up now."

Fiona choked up and couldn't respond for a few seconds. "Some people may think I grew up too fast."

Mrs. Fitzpatrick composed herself. "They may, but some things can't be helped. Anyway, sit and eat."

There were rashers, mushrooms, sliced tomato and mashed potato, all served with porter. The escorts took their meal at the field hands' table, Murphy and Fiona in the dining room. She inclined her head toward him and spoke in a low voice. "The reason our companions are eating in the other room is the less we know about them the better. They don't want us hearing too much."

"Leaving that aside, how are you feeling?"

"In a daze. It's not so painful. I don't feel I'm awake."

When they finished eating Mrs. Fitzpatrick returned to take the dishes away. "As you know we couldn't keep whiskey in the house when your father was alive, not for long anyway. I went and bought a bottle of Jameson's and a bottle of bourbon today. I didn't know what your American would want to drink. They're in the cabinet next to the icebox. I'll be going up in a few minutes. My room is in the other wing, but the beds are all made upstairs."

Fiona smiled. "Thank you, Mrs. Fitzpatrick."

After she left they moved into the living room. Murphy did have a Jameson's. Fiona took her time with the porter. They both sat on the sofa. Fiona intertwined her arm with his and rested her head on his shoulder. "Welcome to my castle."

Murphy peered around the room. The fireplace was large with an enormous wooden mantel. The hearth was made of fieldstone and mortar, like the chimney, and extended into the room. It took Murphy a minute to realize the unusual aroma was caused by burning peat, rather than firewood. There were open dark stained beams running the full width of the ceiling with whitewashed spaces in between. The furniture was upholstered and finished with dark red fabric. A fine carpet lay on the floor with diamond shaped patterns of white and deep blue. *This room, I've never been in anything like it, the warmth of the fire, the nearness of Fiona. Can this be her first time here since she was fifteen years old? How terrible to have been forced to leave. I can't think of a damn thing to say.*

Fiona led Murphy upstairs. He carried both valises. Fiona pointed to the first room on the right. "Yours can go in there, mine in the next room, please. The bathroom is at the end of the hall."

Murphy put the valises in their respective rooms and went into the bathroom. As he passed her room on the way back he said, "Good night, Fiona." He did not hear a response.

He turned out the light and fell asleep quickly but hadn't slept more than fifteen minutes when something awakened him—someone next to him.

Fiona's voice whispered in his ear. "Now you didn't think I was going to let you stay in here alone the first night away from our nosey delegations, did you?"

Daylight crept in the window. *Am I dreaming? Can I be sleeping with Fiona in her ancestral family home*? He stretched his wounded leg.

"Are you awake?" Her head was on his shoulder. Their eyes were only inches apart when his met hers.

"I'm still trying to figure that out. If it's a dream, I don't want to wake up."

She giggled. "It's not a dream, silly, and we should get up. We have a busy day ahead."

They got to the dining room, and Mrs. Fitzpatrick was ready with eggs to poach. There was a pot of tea, and Fiona filled two cups.

Murphy accepted one. "What are our plans anyway?"

"I have to meet with the solicitor, the undertaker and the parish priest, not necessarily in that order. At some point I need to take a tour of the farm, now that I own it, and see if there is anything that needs attention."

Mrs. Fitzpatrick turned from the stove. "If you don't mind my saying so, you should start with Mr. Ryan, the undertaker. It's been several days since your father crossed over. We'd be well neigh finished by now, but for you having to get here from France. I wouldn't delay things any longer."

"Thank you, Mrs. Fitzpatrick, you are quite right."

After breakfast and bathing, Fiona changed into a plain gray skirt with a puffy white blouse, modest by her Paris standards. Murphy put on his uniform. Their escorts from the night before were waiting with the car. This was the first time Murphy had seen Ireland in the daylight. As they rode they passed wide green fields, many of them with grazing cattle. There were tall hedges everywhere. Hills were visible to the north.

They got to Ryan's Funeral Home and were let off. The office was small with a tiled floor of alternating white and brown squares. Ryan was in his late forties, bald and a little overweight. At the sight of Fiona he stiffened but offered them seats in comfortable brown leather chairs. His own chair, behind the desk, was straight backed and webbed. "We shouldn't put things off to long, Miss McDermott. As you know we couldn't do much until you got here."

Fiona squeezed her purse next to her on the chair. "What do you suggest?"

He cleared his throat. "If you don't mind we could do the wake at your home the day after tomorrow, followed by a Requiem Mass and burial. It would give you all day tomorrow to get ready. I suggest a closed coffin. Your father had not been in his best form for a while, but your neighbors will still want him there to say goodbye."

Fiona gave him a slight smile. "It's fine by me, but I want to see him now."

Ryan stood abruptly, gave a half bow, and took them downstairs to the cold basement. He removed the lid from a plain coffin, and Fiona looked inside. As her eyes teared up, Murphy held his breath. Thomas McDermott was dressed in a suit and tie, and his hair was neatly combed. However, his face was rough and lined with veins.

Their next stop was the solicitor, Mr. O'Leary. He was older and thinner than Mr. Ryan. He grinned and held out his hand. "Fiona, I can't believe it's you. It's been so long."

She smiled and took his hand. "Thank you, Mr. O'Leary, and thank you for seeing us without an appointment. This is my friend, Lieutenant George Murphy from the American peace delegation.

"Lieutenant, pleased to meet you." He held out his hand to Murphy.

Murphy shook his hand. "And I you, sir."

"Would you like to see the will? It's simple."

"Please, I would. I thought he might have changed it to leave me out."

Mr. O'Leary sat at his desk. "It was just the opposite. He didn't have a will until two years ago when he came to see me, said he wanted to make sure everything went to you." O'Leary reached into a file folder on his desk and pulled out some papers. "I can give you copies of the will, the letters testamentary, my certificate as executor and a form signed by me in that capacity transferring all bank accounts into your name. You will have to take the last two over to The Bank of Ireland and sign the signature card there. I will prepare an executor's deed transferring the farm into your name. Afterwards, I will make sure it is recorded, and everything will all be in order."

Fiona rose. "Thank you. It's all so sudden. I'm glad you have things so under control."

"There is one more thing."

Fiona sat again and raised an eyebrow. "What is it, Mr. O'Leary?"

"A letter."

"A letter?"

"From your father. He gave it to me only a week before he died and told me to place it in your hands only." He reached into the folder again. "Here it is."

Fiona gazed at the envelope while holding it before she swallowed and placed it in her handbag with the other papers.

Fiona asked to be driven to St. Mary's Church. When they were dropped off, Fiona turned to Murphy. "George, I have to talk with Father Murray on my own. There's a pub around the corner. Why don't you have a drink and come back in about forty minutes? We should be done by then."

Murphy found the pub. There were five men seated at the long dark wooden bar and one rather obese one standing up, who appeared to be lecturing the others. His back was to Murphy and the door. "All I'm saying is we don't want no trollop running one of the biggest farms around." The others were all staring at the door, so he turned around and gaped at Murphy in his American uniform.

Murphy remained calm. *Ignoring this is not an option.* He kept his eyes on the loudmouth and walked up right next to him. "You were saying something about a trollop and a farm, but I don't know the background. Could you fill me in on it, please?"

One of the other men pointed to his jacket. "What's this fancy red, white, and blue ribbon?"

"It's a Silver Star."

"You don't say! How many men did you have to kill to get it?"

Murphy looked right at him and lowered his voice. "I'd rather not say."

At this the heavy man with the big mouth said, "Don't misunderstand me. I'm not talking about anything that's happening here, just about things that happened in other places. But I have to go now anyway. My wife needs me to do some things." He tipped his hat before he left. Murphy accepted a drink from the others.

Fiona entered St. Mary's Church by the main entrance, the first time she had been there since she was a girl. Staring up at the round window, over the gothic ones, above the altar, made it hard for her to swallow.

"Fiona!" Father Murray wore a cassock and walked to her with his arm outstretched. He was grayer than she remembered and a little bent over. "It's wonderful to see you. I always knew you would be back some day."

"Father Murray, it's so good to see you. I feel like I am

stepping back into an enchanted dream. Being away from this church makes me realize how splendid it is."

"It is that. I'm sorry about your father."

"I feel bad I couldn't have been with him at the end."

"Fiona, it's not your fault. None of it is. You were forced out of your home in a society that's not kind to girls on their own."

"No one has been rude to me here, yet, but I suspect there's a lot of gossip."

"There will be. There will always be, but you're doing a lot more for Ireland now than they are. How many of them would receive escorts from both the provisional government and the United States Army?"

"I sent my friend over to Quealy's so we can talk. You say it's not my fault, but it's a long-standing Christian principle that we always have a choice."

"We do, but there's not a soul among us who hasn't made the wrong one at one time or another. God has an enormous capacity for forgiveness, forgiveness that every single one of us needs at some point. Let's have a seat." He took one in the front pew. "Now what about the funeral?"

Fiona sat also. "Mr. Ryan wants to do it the day after tomorrow. I was thinking we can have people at the house from noon to three and do the Mass before the cemetery. Afterward I'm sure people will come back to the house."

"It's a good plan. There's no time to do the old-fashioned three-day wake. You have to get back to Paris."

After Father Murray explained the details, he walked her to the back of the church to the door, where Murphy waited outside.

Fiona waved him over and linked her arm around

his. "Father Murray, this is my friend, Lieutenant George Murphy. He works for the American delegation at the peace conference. George, this is Father Murray. He baptized me."

Father Murray studied Murphy. "Pleased to meet you, Lieutenant Murphy. Fiona told me she sent you over to the pub."

"Yes she did, and I'm pleased to meet you, Father."

"How did the two of you meet?"

"My mentor, Congressman Hamill, introduced me to both Fiona and Sean O'Kelly. Mr. O'Kelly asked me to take Fiona over to introduce her to members of our delegation. I can tell you she made a lot more of an impression on them than I ever did."

Father Murray nodded. "That she would!"

CHAPTER XIV

EARLY TUESDAY MORNING Fiona took her tour of the farm with Eamon Burke, the foreman, and the rest of the day was spent preparing for the funeral especially for the reception at the farmhouse. Mrs. Fitzpatrick offered to purchase the food, but Fiona wanted to undertake the task herself. She said it was about time she engaged the townspeople on public streets. Murphy accompanied her. Their first stop was the fish market where Fiona ordered smoked Atlantic salmon and cooked shrimp to be delivered the next morning. They walked to the butcher. During the walk the people they passed appeared to be avoiding them. No one was outwardly rude. It was more like they didn't want to recognize Fiona. Murphy could only speculate as to whether this was because of her past or because of her present association with the provisional government. When they got to the butcher shop Fiona ordered rashers and sausage also to be delivered the following morning. Murphy noted the butcher was polite and businesslike with Fiona, as was the fishmonger, but while they appeared to recognize her, they did not go out of their way to welcome her home. Did the fact she was there frighten them? Fiona was charming with both of them, but not gushing like she was with Murphy's coworkers at the Hôtel de Crillon. There were subsequent stops at the dairy for butter and cheese, the bakery for bread, and the greengrocer. The pattern remained the same, the merchants being polite, but distant, and the pedestrians pretending they didn't exist until one woman they passed exclaimed, "Fiona? Fiona, it *is* you." She gave Fiona a big hug and exclaimed, "Molly, Molly. Look, it's Fiona."

Molly kept walking but finally turned and stiffened. "Fiona, how good to see you! We understand you're Ireland's principal voice in Paris these days. So sorry about your father."

"Thank you, Mrs. O'Connell, but Sean O'Kelly is our real voice. I'm just someone who also happens to be there, and thank you, Mrs. Lynch. May I introduce my friend Lieutenant George Murphy? George, this is Mrs. Lynch, and this is Mrs. O'Connell. They both taught me at St. Mary's School."

"It's a pleasure, ladies."

They both nodded and Mrs. Lynch spoke. "It's a pleasure to meet you lieutenant. We heard you sent a roadblock scurrying the other night and a loudmouth yesterday."

Fiona waited until they parted before turning to Murphy. "Loudmouth, scurrying, yesterday?"

After he told her what had happened in the pub, she folded her arms. "And you're the man with no self-confidence?"

❧

Molly turned to Mrs. Lynch. "Was that necessary?"

Mrs. Lynch smiled. "Molly, you can't be neutral. You either have to be for her or against her, and when Ireland gets home rule, believe me, you won't want to be the latter."

❧

On the morning of the funeral, the food was being set up. The dining table was big and round with a center pedestal. The surface was an antique green finished with inlaid floral images. The seafood was sitting there on iced trays and had a clean fresh smell. The rashers and sausage were next to the stove in the kitchen, and bottles of beer and stout sat in tubs of ice in the corner of the dining room along with white French wine.

Before Murphy came downstairs Fiona showed him the letter from her father.

Dear Fiona,

My darling daughter, it's hard for me to know where to begin other than to say I'm proud of you. Despite all the bad things I did and the effect they had on you, you have somehow managed not just to survive, but to flourish in the real Ireland, not the British possession. There will be people who will use things you had to do against you. But always remember, they wouldn't do that if they didn't realize you are better than they are. Your mother used to say it was better to knock over a potted plant than to go unnoticed. You learned from her well. You always make your point. I'm sorry it was through my fault we stopped having a father-daughter relationship. It's too late for me to change it. You will be left well set up though. I may have drunk too much, but I didn't gamble. Eamon kept the farm running, and I ask you to keep him on. The bank accounts are in good order. While you continue with your diplomacy, the estate will run itself and should be able to provide whatever you will need. It's about all I can do for you now. I won't deceive myself that you inherited any of your talent from me. You're your mother. Oh, how I miss her.

But there's more to tell you, and please take it seriously. You are in danger! I would write to you in Paris and tell you not to come to my funeral, whenever that will be, but there's little chance my letter would ever make it out of Ireland, and, knowing you, you'd come anyway. Don't believe whatever the authorities will say is my cause of death. Be sure to speak to Dr. Maloney to see if it's consistent with my medical history. If it's not, then my death will have been timed to get you here for something they have planned. I won't tell you what to do. You will come up with something better than whatever I could suggest!

With love and prayers,

Daa

George lifted his eyes from the letter. "Fiona—"

"Not now, George."

"But, Fiona—"

"Not now!"

By twelve o'clock everything was ready, and people began arriving. Mr. Ryan had the closed coffin placed next to the fireplace. Most stopped by it and said a silent prayer. Murphy and Fiona stood a little past the coffin to greet people. *Why do all these people want to talk to us at the farmhouse when almost no one acknowledged us on the street?*

St. Mary's Church was so crowded the funeral party from the farmhouse had trouble squeezing inside.

Father Murray led the processional with four altar boys, one holding a high crucifix, two with lit candles and one with an incense burner. Fiona took Murphy's arm to walk up the aisle, behind the coffin. The organ music filled the church as did the smoke from the incense.

About twenty people came back to the farmhouse after the service at the cemetery.

A woman came up to Murphy and introduced herself. "My husband was at Quealy's the day before yesterday when the inappropriate comment was made. You handled it well. It gave the man a chance to back off without looking any more foolish than he already did. I say this because I don't want there to be any ongoing bad feelings. He was afraid to come here but he was at the church."

"Thank you, and good manners require me to accept his explanation that he was talking about someone else." He saw Fiona beckoning.

There was an elderly man in a gray suit standing with her. "Dr. Maloney, this is my friend, Lieutenant George Murphy. George, this is Dr. Maloney, my father's physician." After the men shook hands Fiona turned back to the doctor. "Dr. Maloney, would you please tell George what you just told me?"

The doctor harrumphed. "According to the official death certificate, which I did not prepare, the cause of Mr. McDermott's death was cirrhosis of the liver."

Murphy gestured with his hand. "Wouldn't that be consistent with his drinking habits?"

"Most people will think so, but I'm not one of them."

"Why not?"

"I examined him a month ago. There was no jaundice, and his urine test was normal. Whatever killed him, it wasn't his liver."

Murphy's head snapped back. "What did?"

The doctor straightened up. "I don't know, and someone is making sure it stays that way."

Fiona turned to Murphy. "We're leaving first thing in the morning."

Only Murphy's eyes moved. "Good idea!"

The next morning they packed into the car with their two escorts and headed back toward Dublin. As they were passing a hedgerow, they spotted two police cars ahead. The elder escort turned and gave Fiona a somber look. They slowed down. When they got closer they observed a body lying in the roadway and, next to it, a rifle. The dead man had a large open head wound and another small round one on his chest. An officer signaled them to stop. Fiona turned to Murphy. "You better handle this."

He got out and walked up to the sergeant in charge. "What happened?"

The officer grimaced. "That's what we're trying to determine. The victim wasn't shot here. The blood is all on the other side of the hedgerow. Whoever shot him dragged the body and the rifle out here so that we would find them. It looks like the dead man was lying in wait for someone when he was ambushed himself."

Murphy glanced at the field. "What could he have been planning?"

The policeman cocked his head. "Lieutenant Murphy, we know who you are. He was obviously waiting to shoot Miss McDermott, but someone else got him first."

"Who could that someone be?"

The officer sniffed. "I would like to say it was Irish Republicans, but it obviously wasn't. They would have taken the rifle, not left it here to create a scene!"

CHAPTER XV

THE NEXT MORNING Murphy was in the Hôtel de Crillon, catching up on his invoices. Stephen Brown marched over to his desk. "Have you heard about Richard?"

"Richard? No. What do you mean?"

Stephen pressed his fists on the desk. "He's been accused of misappropriating funds. He allegedly paid for travel that never occurred and received kickbacks. The news broke with an article in *Paris Aujour'hui* by Henri Durand. Durand found a secret account in the name of Richard Ambrose at *Banque Nationale de Crédit*. It contained thousands of francs, and all the deposits were made this year."

Murphy jumped up from his chair. "Richard would never do that, and anything that started with an investigation by Henri Durand has to be fake. I've had the benefit of seeing that firsthand myself."

"Anyway, Ambassador White wants to talk with you about it. He said to send you up as soon as you got here."

Murphy flung the invoice he was translating onto the desk

and went to the elevator. He was shown into White's office as soon as he arrived. The ambassador lifted his head from what he was writing but still kept pen in hand. "I'm glad to see you're back. We have a bigger problem here right now. How much do you know about the Richard Ambrose matter?"

"Only that he's been accused of misappropriation of funds based on an article by Henri Durand."

White dropped his pen and reclined in his chair. "Please take a seat. These were United States federal funds, so our government has the jurisdiction to prosecute him, but so do the French, since the crime is alleged to have occurred here. He is not travelling on a diplomatic passport, but they would probably defer to us to avoid any situation which could affect the conference. But our ability to act is circumscribed."

Murphy sank into the chair. "What is the reason, sir?"

"First of all we're diplomats, not law enforcement officers. We can't prosecute anybody. We have a status of forces agreement with France which defers all prosecution of American military personnel to our judge advocate, but Mr. Ambrose is a civilian. The only United States agency that would have the power to charge him would be the Justice Department, and they don't have any staff in France. So, what do we do? If we bring a federal prosecutor here from Washington, it will become a major news event and will interfere with the peace conference."

Murphy lifted his hands. "Aren't there any other alternatives?"

"There are. We could ship Mr. Ambrose back to Washington to face charges there, away from the French press."

Murphy stiffened. "But, sir, if Richard is innocent, as

I believe he is, he will need evidence to back it up which is available only here."

White cast his eyes downward for a few seconds. "Do you know what the Camorra is?"

Murphy's head jerked. "Isn't it a criminal organization that moved to New York from Italy? What could it possibly have to do with this?"

White took a deep breath. "Mr. Ambrose's grandfather came to the United States with those people. Richard has a clean record himself, but some of his relatives don't. I don't believe in holding it against him, but there are people in the Justice Department who have different ideas."

"No, no, it's not right. What can I do?"

White sat back. "You mentioned some evidence would be available only here. Durand, in his article, cited records from the *Banque Nationale de Crédit*. If this had happened in the United States we would have no trouble getting copies of the records, but in France, we're stymied. You seem to have become our go between with French law enforcement. See if your contacts can get the bank records the Justice Department will need, but remember, you're acting as a diplomat. Don't cross the line."

"I won't, sir!"

❧

The ambassador didn't say that Murphy couldn't talk to Richard, nor did Murphy ask. He arranged to meet him at the café on Rue de Rivoli. They ordered a carafe of red wine, and Murphy went straight to the subject at hand. "How did you find out about these accusations?"

Richard exhaled. "The same way you found out about some of your incidents, the newspaper. If I had known I had all this money, I would have rented a bigger apartment."

The voice from behind jarred them. "A bigger apartment you say!" It was Henri Durand with a big grin.

Murphy spun around. "He said if he had the money, which he does not. But you know what? How about if we answer a few questions for you if you answer some for us?" Was it the wine making him do this?

Durand sniffed. "I thought I put a lot in the article."

"But not how you happened to come across these *Banque Nationale de Crédit* records?"

"I certainly wasn't trolling through bank files on the chance I might find something, nor could I. Obviously I was tipped off."

"By whom?"

Durand grunted. "If I revealed my source, to you, I'd never get another tip for the rest of my remaining short career."

Murphy slapped his hand on the table. "Okay, you can still tell us how much was in the account at *Banque Nationale de Crédit*? When was the last deposit? Have there been any withdrawals?"

Durand shrugged. "D'accord, there were over fourteen thousand francs in the account. The last deposit was four days ago. There have not been withdrawals." He glared at Richard. "Now tell me, Monsieur Ambrose, when did you open the account?"

Richard threw his head back and grunted. "I didn't. I didn't even know it existed until I read about it in your article."

Durand removed a pencil and pad from his pocket and extended his neck toward Richard. "Why pay the travel agent for two round trips between Marseille and New York for Mr. Waters and Mr. Dolan when neither of them has left Paris since the conference started?"

"I only paid for one voyage here for both of them."

"Thank you. We will talk again." Durand stood, gave a little smile, put his writing utensils away and walked to the door.

Murphy turned to Richard. "How do you process the checks?"

"I write the name of the payee and the amount and give them to Madame Hardy. She passes them on to the bursar who puts them through the check writing machine. They come back to me. I sign them and mail them out."

"So, you cannot send out a check without two other people processing it?"

Richard nodded. "I could not."

"It's helpful, but more important is that all the checks are done on a check writing machine. Excuse me for not knowing about it, but I don't send out checks. I just approve invoices. From what I do understand there are lots of different types of check writing machines, each of which has its own unique way of forming numerals and symbols."

Richard folded his hands on the table. "You're right. They're all in one elaborate script style or another."

"If we can get a look at the cancelled checks, we can tell what type of machine it was done on and who uses it. What bank were the checks drawn on?"

"*Riggs National Bank* in Washington."

"Do they send you the cancelled checks?"

"No, it would be difficult to do it transatlantic."

Murphy plunked his hands on the table. "Can't you get them to make an exception under the circumstances?"

"I'll have to get someone else to send a transatlantic cablegram. I'm not welcome in the office now."

Murphy hesitated. "Is it just because of this allegation?"

It took Richard a few seconds. "The fact that you asked that question answers it. No one here worried about my family's history before the article came out!"

৵

Murphy had arranged to meet Fiona for dinner that evening. She was to be in his neighborhood on business anyway. After they took their seats in the café, and wine was served, Murphy took a swig and swallowed hard to build up his nerve. "Can we talk?" He gulped.

She stared back at him. "Of course. What is it?"

"We were essentially living together in your house. I escorted you up and down the aisle at you father's funeral and stood next to you at the wake to accept condolences. Most people take that to mean a serious relationship."

She lifted her head. "It does that."

"Fiona, I want to marry you."

Fiona squeezed her eyes shut, but somehow a tear still escaped. It was almost a full minute before she responded. "Oh, George, George, George, if my past were not what it was, if I were not so totally committed to Irish freedom that nothing else matters, if I were capable of living a normal life and, most importantly of all, if I expected to live long enough for it to matter, I would jump at your offer, but we both know none of those things are true, and I cannot."

"Fiona, your past shows me only how brave and resourceful you are. I support and extol your commitment to Ireland and will do everything in my power to keep you alive for a long, long time."

She took his hand in both of hers and kissed it before shaking her head!

CHAPTER XVI

MURPHY WALKED TO the préfecture Monday morning. *Why am I doing this? Is it to get the information Ambassador White wants? Am I going further than the ambassador wants? He warned me not to cross the line, but where is the line? He told me to make a diplomatic request for bank records, but what if they lead to something else? Can I follow up on it even after White reminded me I'm not a law enforcement officer?*

The commissaire offered Murphy a seat. He took it. "Are you interested in the Richard Ambrose matter?"

Trudeau shook his head. "No, even though it happened on French soil, and we have jurisdiction, we believe it is more your concern than ours."

Murphy persisted, "While our courts have jurisdiction to conduct a trial, they do not have the authority to require French banks to produce records of transactions which occurred here. Would you be able to get any of those records for us?"

"What records are you looking for?"

Murphy reviewed his own notes. "We want to see the monthly statements listing all deposits and withdrawals from the *Banque Nationale de Crédit* account, although Mr. Durand says there are none of the latter. Most important is that we get to see the signature card from when the account was opened. We would prefer the original, but if we can't have it, a clear photograph of the document."

"Let me see what I can do."

After leaving the Préfecture de Police, Murphy walked back to the Hôtel de Crillon. It wasn't the same without Richard. Would Trudeau get the signature card? Would Richard's contact get the cancelled checks? The last part did exceed what the ambassador had authorized. The Justice Department didn't need Murphy to get records from a bank in their own backyard, but Murphy wanted to see those checks himself. Was he putting his own position at risk?

When Murphy arrived at his office he spotted Stephen motionless staring at a paperweight on his desk with a blank face. He walked over to him. "Are you in a hypnotic trance?"

Stephen raised his head. "I wish I were. I guess you haven't heard."

"Haven't heard what?"

"Richard was arrested last night by a deputy United States marshal."

Murphy stiffened. "What? Where did he take him? Can I see him?"

Stephen stood. "Too late. The deputy marshal brought

him directly to a ship in Marseilles. It sailed for New York this morning."

Murphy's head was shaking. "Something's not right here. No one's going to go to that much trouble for a run-of-the-mill embezzlement case. That level of intercontinental prosecution would normally be reserved for multi-million dollar cases or matters of national security."

Stephen sat again. "Or those involving organized crime."

"But Richard isn't involved with those members of his family."

"The Justice Department thinks otherwise!"

❧

Fiona walked to the Metro station on her way to the Majestic Hôtel, headquarters of the British delegation. *Captain Sanders offered to help, and it looks like I need it.*

She looked around as she boarded a train. *Am I imagining things? Did a tall man watch me get on the train? He waited to board until after I did.* She got off at the Kléber station. *He is following me.* As she crossed Avenue Kléber and turned right toward the Majestic Hôtel she saw him from the corner of her eye. *He no longer has his guard mustache, but it is the face I saw in the car window on the Champs-Élysées.* As she entered the hotel, she encountered Captain Sanders in the lobby.

He offered his hand. "Miss McDermott, to what do I owe the pleasure?"

She inclined her head toward the window. "Do you see the man across the street, wearing the brown jacket with an open shirt? He's standing next to the tree near the café. He no longer has his guard mustache, but that's him, the one that shot at me, undoubtedly the man who called himself Major Bennett. He followed me here."

Sanders raced to the door. As he came out of the hotel, Bennett took off. There was too much traffic on Avenue Kléber for Sanders to get across in time, so Bennett got away. As Sanders came back to the lobby, everyone there was staring at him and at Fiona.

Sanders shook his head and frowned. "I'm sorry I couldn't catch him but, at least I know what he looks like now. That alone could be a big help."

An older man in a British army uniform approached them "What's all this about, Sanders?"

"That, sir, was the man who called himself Major Bennett, pretended he was from MI5 and fired a shot at Miss McDermott on the Champs-Élysées. He followed her here. Miss McDermott, this is Colonel Johnson, our chief of security."

Fiona held out her hand. "It is an honor to meet you, colonel. You are shouldering such enormous responsibility."

He took her hand. "And it is a pleasure to meet you, Miss McDermott. I am well familiar with your troubles. More importantly for now, this incident is proof positive the scoundrel was not one of ours. We may have our political differences, miss, but we would never tolerate anything like what this wretch has done."

"Thank you, colonel." She smiled at him.

After Johnson left Sanders turned to Fiona. "Should we have a little chat over a cup of tea?"

"That is why I came here in the first place. Bennett's appearance was a surprise."

They sat and Sanders ordered the tea.

Fiona folded her hands in her lap. "Did you hear what happened in Ireland?"

"We did. In fact we have even more information that you should be made aware of."

She put her cup down. "I'm listening."

He leaned forward. "The French police had given us a copy of the signature of the bullet fired at you on the Champs-Élysées."

She picked up her pastry. "How thoughtful of them, but why is that important?"

"Because it matches the signature of the bullet that killed your would-be assassin in Ireland."

She dropped her pastry onto the plate. "What? Are you telling me that the person who shot at me here in Paris might have saved my life in Ireland? That makes no sense."

He sat back. "The only way it does make sense is if the shooter is obsessed with where and how you are killed. Your being murdered in Ireland by a unionist assassin might not suit his purposes."

Fiona unclasped her hands and leaned back. "I was already having trouble believing that the two attacks on me, one by a man pretending to be one of you and the other by a man pretending to be a German diplomat, were coincidences. More and more now it seems they were not. The sniper in Ireland could have been written off as a continuation of a long-standing conflict, but the matching bullets changes all of that."

Sanders nodded slowly. "And now the person responsible follows you here!"

ঌ

A parcel came for Murphy from *Riggs National Bank.* It contained photographs of all the cancelled checks made payable to the travel agent that calendar year. It was apparent many of the checks were written on a check writing machine other than the one used at Hôtel de Crillon. Not only were the numerals formed differently, but the ink was a darker shade. The account number on those checks was the one used by the delegation travel office, but the individual check numbers bore no relation to those being used by the delegation. Also, none of the suspect checks were deposited in the bank used by the travel agency, but in the *Banque de France* instead.

As Murphy was putting the documents away Madame Hardy advised him police Lieutenant Coderre was there to see him. Murphy rose to greet him. "Good morning Lieutenant Coderre, what can I do for you?"

"It is I who have things for you." He presented Murphy with a package containing the signature card from the account at *Banque Nationale de Crédit* opened in Richard's name, another signature card from the account at *Banque de France*, opened in the name of the travel agency, monthly statements from both accounts and cancelled checks from the *Banque de France* account.

As he looked them over, it became clear the bogus checks from *Riggs National Bank* in Washington were deposited in the *Banque de France* account. Checks were then drawn on that account, and the full amount deposited in the *Banque Nationale de Credit* account in Richard's name. Nothing was paid to anyone else, so the funds never passed through the travel agency, nor did it receive any kickbacks.

As far as Richard's purported involvement was concerned, the signature card at *Banque Nationale de Credit* looked like a good copy of his handwriting, but nothing more. All of the documents from *Banque de France* including the checks were in a different name and signed by someone else.

Murphy put the documents back in the folder and stared at the ceiling. "Whoever signed the card at *Banque Nationale de Crédit* probably had a copy of Richard Ambrose's handwriting to work with, but it's not a terribly close match. More importantly Richard knew what sequence of check numbers the delegation was using. The person who ordered these checks did not. We also know some other person must have been involved since the *Banque de France* documents were signed by a different party, using a different name." They were both still standing. Murphy offered Coderre a chair.

He took the seat across from Murphy. "It is most curious. Every misappropriated franc ended up in this phony Ambrose account. It profited no one. There was no motive except to implicate Monsieur Ambrose." He placed his hands on Murphy's desk and leaned forward. "Since this no longer appears to be an internal matter for your delegation, Commissaire Trudeau directed me to inform you we are taking over the investigation. Our division would normally not get involved in this type of crime. We would leave it to regular detectives, but since it involves the peace conference it has a higher priority."

Murphy sat silent. *What should I do now? Does this mean Richard is exonerated? But he's already on a ship to New York.*

Having gone this far, they're not going to release him without something more definitive. Ambassador White warned me not to cross the line. How much trouble can I get into by not dropping it? He shifted his attention back to Coderre. "Can we still keep these records?"

"The commissaire would not have sent me with them otherwise."

Murphy stood up and began pacing back and forth. "If you can find the check writing machine that did the bogus checks you would probably have the case solved."

The lieutenant maintained a poker face. "I know."

Murphy sat on the edge of his desk. "Would you accompany me to the travel agency to whom these checks were made payable?"

Coderre stood. "Of course, but I should let you know they have already been questioned, and, as you know, they did not get any of the money."

They walked several blocks to the agency where they asked to see the manager. Wherever the line was Ambassador White told him not to cross, this was beyond it. After Coderre showed his police ID, and introductions were made, the manager invited them to sit. Murphy explained why they were there. The manager had a stack of papers on his desk which he continued to study.

Murphy interrupted. "How often do you deposit the checks you receive?"

The manager raised his head. "Checks? Oh, we make deposits every day. Sometimes they may sit here overnight, but never more than twenty-four hours."

Murphy put a hand on the desk. "How many of the delegations do you book travel for?"

The manager sat back and snapped, "Most of them."

"How many checks do you have here now?"

"Thirty or forty."

"Can we see them?"

The man turned his head away and lifted his chin. "I'm not allowed to show you confidential client information."

Coderre slapped his hand on the desk. "Since this no longer appears to be an internal matter for the American delegation, it is now in police hands. It will be easier for you to show us the checks than to have us seize them as evidence. In the latter case it will be some months before the case is concluded, and we can return them to you."

The manager jumped to his feet, and removed the checks from the safe. Murphy had brought the photos of the cancelled checks from *Riggs National Bank* with him. Both he and Coderre compared the checks from the safe to the photos, looking only at the lines done by the various check writing machines. They found a dead ringer. Everything lined up: the dark shade, the formation of the numerals, even the lettering preceding them. The printing on the check read, *DELEGATION VON DEUTSCHLAND.*

Murphy held the check up to the manager's face. "Was this sent to you by the German delegation?"

The man closed the safe. "It was sent to us by one of the groups who refer to themselves as the German delegation."

⁂

Murphy had arranged to meet Claude at the French Army Museum on the Left Bank, off Avenue de Tourville. He entered through the Tomb of Napoleon where he admired the golden dome and three levels of stone columns in front. Claude was not yet there, so Murphy proceeded to the cobblestone courtyard in back near Hôtel des Invalides where he studied the old muzzle loaded cannons. An Arab man approached him. "I recognize you from the newspaper. You are Lieutenant Murphy. Is that not so?"

Murphy turned toward him. "It is so."

"Permit me to have a word. I am Egyptian. Your Irish girlfriend would appreciate my position. It is hard to represent a country at this conference when the British say you are not a country at all, but only a segment of their empire. It is even worse when their prime minister is one of the only four people here who are allowed to decide anything. We fought beside the British at Siwa, Sollum and Mersa. Now they pretend they don't know us."

Murphy turned to face him "It is a big problem here. President Wilson thought we were entering the war to establish a new world order of national self-determination. Now the only changes we see are the parceling out of land from one empire to another. Colonies are not obtaining their freedom, but only new and different masters."

As Claude arrived it began to rain, so he and Murphy rushed back into the grand tomb where they sat on a bench behind the marble rail overlooking the sarcophagus. Murphy rested his hands on the seat. "How was class today?"

"Interesting, but it is not why I wanted to talk with you, mon ami. Whatever is this thing that happened with Richard Ambrose?"

Murphy told him everything, including what happened at the travel agency. "Once Ambassador White got word to the Justice Department about the German check writing machine, they had no choice but to order his release. So, he's getting a short visit home."

Claude couldn't control his smirk. "So, we're back to where we started out. It had to be the Germans!"

Murphy gulped. "I should have realized. I'm not sure what got me off track. Maybe it was the phony MI5 officer, but now it appears he's in cahoots with Herr Ostomeyer and the mystery man, both of whom appear to be German?"

"Mon ami, the one thing we know with absolute certainty is the check writing machine and the plot to frame Richard were both German. When you add it to Herr Ostomeyer and the mystery man, it leads us to one conclusion." Claude rubbed his forehead. "But something is not right, mon ami. We are looking at this from the wrong direction."

Murphy huffed. "Is there a right direction?"

Claude waved his hand. "We have to go back right to the beginning."

Murphy spread his hands. "What is the beginning?"

"The beginning, mon ami, was when Angeline first came up to you in the café."

"Okay, so what?" Murphy stood.

Claude gestured downward with his hands. "What reason did she give for wanting to talk to you?"

Murphy shrugged his shoulders. "She said she wanted me to introduce her to Congressman Hamill."

"Why?"

"So that he could get President Wilson to listen to her about Belgium." Claude just fixed Murphy with a blank stare until Murphy's head snapped back. "Oh, yeah! I get it. That's not likely! Is it?"

"George, chiefs of state, other than Lloyd George,

Clemenceau and Orlando, can't get to talk to Wilson now. Claude stood up and paced back and forth. "Which came first, your involvement with Angeline or your participation in the investigation of the phony crime wave?"

Murphy propped himself against the marble rail. "My assignment to the crime wave came first, but I met Angeline before taking any real action. It would be unlikely for anyone to know about it. More importantly, she first contacted you two weeks earlier, even before I knew about the assignment."

Claude smacked his fist into his hand. "So, mon ami, we have to accept Angeline's interest in you was triggered by something else, so what was her real motive? Why did she come to you in the first place?"

"I don't have a clue!"

CHAPTER XVII

MURPHY WAS AT the Hôtel de Crillon preparing to catch up on his invoices when Madame Hardy told him a woman was there to see him, a woman who would give her name only as Martine. Murphy said to show her in. Did this mean she had a tip for him? When she arrived he brought her right over to his desk "What can I do for you?"

Her eyes swept around the whole salon. "May I sit?"

He gestured at the empty chair. "Of course."

She folded her hands in her lap and sat up straight. "I have information for you about the woman you called Angeline."

Murphy had to constrain himself from jumping out of his chair. "That's the most interesting thing I've heard in a long series of interesting things."

She handed him a large photo. "Look at this." The photo showed the front steps of a school in Brussels with about twenty girls in school uniforms. They all appeared to be about ten or eleven years old. "This photo was taken in 1906. Look at the girl on the extreme left of the second row."

Murphy's face froze. "Oh my God! It looks like a young Angeline."

Martine smiled. "It is. Now look at the caption with her name."

"Natasha Volkov?" He gazed back at Martine with his mouth still open.

Martine sat back. "Yes, Natasha was born in Brussels. Her father was a Russian diplomat. The family returned to Russia three years after this picture was taken, but Natasha had spent the first fourteen years of her life in Belgium, which was why it was so easy for her to impersonate a Belgian woman."

"That's why my friend Claude Bisset was convinced by her accent."

Martine allowed herself a slight smile. "Undoubtedly. In Russia she began to associate with other young people aligned with the Bolsheviks. She became a full-fledged Bolshevik herself. Her special talent was luring aristocrats and czarist government officials into compromising situations which could be used against them."

"Why did you go to so much trouble to find this out?"

"Lieutenant Murphy, I thought I made it clear to you how vital it was to me to make sure what did happen in Belgium was accurately set forth. When a phony like her tells fake stories of her own involvement, it creates a false trail and threatens to destroy everything I work for. Her lies sabotaged our credibility."

"What was she doing with me, here in Paris?"

"Considering how you met, she was certainly acting under orders from her Bolshevik controllers. What her purpose was is still vague."

"Who killed her? Was it one of her previous victims?"

"That is unlikely. It is more likely that you were the immediate target for a frame-up, but you could not have been the ultimate target. I don't mean to offend you, but you are not important enough to justify this level of operation."

Murphy looked away. "I already knew that. What was their real goal?"

"Even I don't know. What I can tell you though is, as much as I hate the Germans, they are not the ones after you. It is the Bolsheviks!"

Sean O'Kelly listened carefully as Murphy explained what Martine had told him. They were both seated in the lobby of the Grand Hotel. When Murphy finished O'Kelly clasped his own hands on his lap. "You were right to come here and tell me this. It explains much."

Murphy looked back at him. "Not to me."

"George, there is much going on in Ireland now. You could call it a state of war. There may be no battles between big armies, but there is a lot of shooting and killing."

"I've seen that firsthand."

O'Kelly lifted his hands back up. "I know you have, but there are more players than you may realize."

"How so?"

O'Kelly put his glasses in his jacket pocket. "The nationalists want independence from Britain, although there are some who would settle for home rule within the British Empire. Then we have the unionists who want to stay with Britain."

Murphy spread his hands. "I know all that, but what does it have to do with Bolsheviks?"

O'Kelly sighed. "There isn't a conflict anywhere in Europe now that the Soviets haven't stuck their noses into, and Ireland is no exception. In February they took over a mental asylum in Monaghan and hoisted a red flag over it. Even armed police weren't able to dislodge them."

Murphy shook his head. "I wasn't aware of that, but what does any of this have to do with Fiona?"

"George, the Soviets are obsessed with taking over the Irish nationalist movement but, so far, have had little success. Most of our leaders want nothing to do with them. Fiona is a major bane to the Soviets. She's prominent, popular and attracts people to the nationalist side, especially the trade unions. The working class can appreciate what she had to do after her alienation from her family. She became our most effective contact with them. All the Bolsheviks care about is that she is adamantly opposed to Communism and, to put the candle on the cake, is now also a landowner."

"Then why would they save her from a sniper?"

O'Kelly groaned. "Because the sniper was obviously one of the people they hate even more, a unionist. They could not let the unionists have that victory. Were they to prevail, and Ireland remain in the United Kingdom, the soviets would be wasting their time there. Also, killing Fiona would not alienate the unionist's own base."

Murphy shook his head. "So they want to get credit for killing her?"

"No, no, they just don't want the unionists to profit from it. They may want to avoid being openly involved.

Remember their purpose is to win over the nationalists. Being blamed for Fiona's death will not help that. More likely they will try to point a finger at someone else."

"Like me?"

O'Kelly nodded. "It could happen that way."

Murphy walked back to the Hôtel Continental trying to absorb what he'd just been told. Fiona's situation and his were far more dire even than what he had believed. The British, even those whose affiliation with the government was faked, had some limits as to what they could do without alienating people they wanted to win over. But the Russians, the Soviet ones, the Bolsheviks had no such constraints. They cared for nothing and nobody, let alone what the rest of the world would think. What had happened to his nice easy job of translating invoices? This was like being back in the trenches!

Madame Hardy didn't greet Murphy when he entered the office area at the Hôtel de Crillon. "Ambassador White needs you now."

He wasted no time getting upstairs. White invited him to sit. "Lieutenant Murphy, I need you to undertake another errand."

Murphy sat straight. "Of course, sir. What would it be?"

White took a folder out of his briefcase and opened it on the desk. "It has to do with Alsace-Lorraine. Clemenceau is adamant it be returned to France since it was seized by Germany at the end of the 1870 Franco-Prussian War."

Murphy shrugged his shoulders. "Not a surprise, sir."

"The Germans are objecting, saying for most of its history, the territory was a part of Germany, not France, the people there are German and want to stay with Germany. They claim that the only reason the area was French prior to 1870 was it was seized during the French Revolution."

Murphy squirmed in his seat. "Do we have an official position on it, sir?"

White pushed his chair back. "Both sides argue that, according to President Wilson's Fourteen Points, the will of the people there should control. Of course, it's not so simple."

Murphy blinked. "What do the French say?"

"When the French army entered the city at the end of this war, it was greeted by cheering crowds, which the French say is all the proof they need the residents want French government. There is little doubt the French are going to prevail on this."

Murphy sat still. *I'm no diplomat. What do I know about international affairs? My only experience with foreign transactions consists of exchanging artillery fire.* "What can we accomplish, at this point, sir?"

"We need to know what the conditions are there before giving our consent. It would look bad for us, for the president, in the newspapers, if we agree to the transfer only to later learn we missed an obvious problem. Both versions are unavoidably biased. I want you to go and see what's happening firsthand. Can you do it?"

Murphy face went blank. *This is an important undertaking, far more than approving invoices for payment. But what about Fiona? Shouldn't she be my chief concern? How great is her risk in Paris? But I'm not really being asked. I'm being told.* He lifted his chin. "I can, sir."

White closed a file on his desk. "How do you plan to proceed?"

Murphy swallowed hard. "The area is under French military rule now. One can learn a lot by observing the demeanor of the people. Are they going about their daily business normally? Do they appear to be content? Is anyone leaving chalk messages on the walls? Are there any posters? Are there many arrests? Are there any protests? Beyond those I can strike up conversations with locals in cafés, restaurants and shops."

White smiled at him. "A good approach, far better than trying to talk to the authorities. Were you to do the latter, I'm sure someone would cherry-pick what you get to see and hear. It's also why you were chosen for this mission. You're low profile enough your activities are likely to go unnoticed. A more seasoned statesman would be easily recognized and monitored. There's something else."

"Sir?"

"It would be a big help to have some photographs."

Murphy stiffened. "Photographs of what, sir?"

"The French have already distributed numerous photos of their troops marching into the city, of the ceremonies that attended it, awards of medals in public squares and the like, but those don't tell us anything. What we do need are pictures of exactly what you referred to a few moments ago: people, shops, streets, everyday life, not staged ceremonies."

Murphy smiled. "I can do that, sir."

"Just make certain you don't photograph any military installations. The war is not officially over yet. There's only an armistice, and the Germans are threatening to withdraw from that because of the way they're being treated here.

Were they to launch another attack, Strasbourg would likely be their first target. The French are all too conscious of this and well prepared should it occur. Do not, I repeat, do not take pictures of any of those preparations."

"I won't, sir."

"My secretary will give you a camera on the way out. Can you leave tomorrow?"

As much as he feared for Fiona's safety, Murphy realized the question was rhetorical!

Fiona was to take all her meals at the Grand Hôtel unless she was escorted by someone who could provide her with some level of protection. *Should I do what I was told? The Hôtel Scribe is directly across the street, and I need a change of scenery.* She walked to the corner of Boulevard des Capucines, crossed the street and entered the Scribe. It was the earlier part of dinner time, so she had no trouble getting a small table. The floor of the restaurant was polished marble with maroon carpeting under the tables. The ceiling was supported by multiple thick square columns with fine cream colored wood finishing and candlelike light fixtures on each of their four faces. Between the columns hung elaborate crystal chandeliers. As she was just about to take her seat, she heard a voice from the next table, "Miss McDermott, are you alone?" It was Captain Sanders.

She turned toward him. "I am that."

He stood. "Would it be an imposition if I asked you to join me?"

What did he want? To continue their previous dialogue?

A business meeting? Was he looking for a date? Was she maintaining her contacts, the way she was supposed to? She flashed a broad smile. "It would not be an imposition, captain. I will, of course, join you."

He held out a chair for her. "Please call me Ted."

"And please call me Fiona." She took the seat he offered.

He resumed his own place. "Thank you, Fiona. It's a fair name. It suits you."

She smirked back.

Fiona ordered the pollack, Sanders the wild boar. They shared a bottle of Chablis Grand Cru. Afterwards they both had espresso. Fiona took a sip. "The food is one of the things I like best about Paris."

Sanders took his cup and rested against the back of the chair. "What did you eat in Ireland?"

"At home my favorites were lamb and salmon. My mother was a good cook. The shellfish in Ireland is also exceptional. Most foreigners don't realize it. The water is warm on the southwest coast of Ireland because of the Gulf Stream, so we get shrimp and scallops that countries so far north don't usually. How about you?"

"Roast beef and Yorkshire Pudding is popular. So is steak and kidney pie. Have you been to many of the Paris restaurants?"

She gave a little snicker. "More than a few, usually without the complications of my last visit to Maxim's. The delegation wants to keep me confined now. They'll probably be annoyed I crossed the street to come here."

"I should walk you home anyway. Maybe they'll think you were escorted the whole time?"

She smiled. "That would be nice." She dropped her eyes.

When he asked for the check she reached for her purse. He held up his hand. "I'll take care of it."

"You shouldn't do that. You didn't invite me to dinner."

He took out his wallet. "I asked you to sit with me, which amounts to the same thing."

When they got outside he offered her his arm, which she took. Once they were inside the Grand Hôtel, he bid her a cordial good-night and left.

Fiona returned to her room. *What happened tonight? It was no business meeting. There was almost no discussion of my incidents. It was a date. What will George be up to in Alsace?*

CHAPTER XVIII

MURPHY GULPED DOWN a small bottle of red wine with his ham and cheese sandwich on the train. *What is Fiona doing back in Paris? Is she safe? What am I doing on this damned train instead of in Paris looking out for her?*

He was only able to get as far as Châlons-sur-Marne before having to switch his mode of transportation, as the final leg of track into Strasbourg had been destroyed by artillery fire and had yet to be repaired. After stepping off the railroad car he was greeted by a man in his mid-thirties dressed in the trousers, cap and heavy shirt of a French workman. When he spoke, it was clear he was an American. "Lieutenant Murphy?"

"Yes!" Murphy was carrying a valise.

"I've been sent to drive you to Strasbourg. I know my appearance is less than military, but I understand we're not supposed to be noticeable. It's not top secret or anything, but we don't want to advertise who we are. We don't want anyone realizing we're American soldiers. It would cause the people in charge to keep an eye on you. My truck's over here." It had no conspicuous markings on it. "I've been told to take you to the Hôtel Rohan, near the cathedral. There'll be a reservation in the name of George Murphy. Three days are paid for. I will pick you up at ten am to return you here unless I hear otherwise. How does that all sound?"

Murphy threw his valise in the back of the truck and got in the passenger side. "It appears that everything is well organized." Murphy knew what to do in Strasbourg, all the things he suggested to Ambassador White. The Germans considered Alsace-Lorraine to be one territory, while the French considered Alsace and Lorraine to be two separate departments. Murphy recalled Joan of Arc was from Lorraine.

Navigating the streets of the medieval inner part of Strasbourg was no easy task. There were not many cars, but streets in the Middle Ages were not designed to enable even one truck trying to get around cars and horses. When they finally got to the Hôtel Rohan, Murphy got out, fetched his valise and told the soldier he would see him in three days.

Once he was settled Murphy visited a bookstore on Rue des Orfévres, a narrow street with storefront businesses at the ground level. The proprietor was an elderly Frenchman wearing glasses with small round frames. "Monsieur, over the centuries Alsatians have learned to live with both countries. For much of our history we were independent. Anyone over forty-eight years of age here experienced the last French rule, which was smooth."

Murphy took out a pen and paper. "What about after the Germans took over in 1871?"

The man returned a book to a shelf. "Things were not

bad, but once this last war broke out, it changed." He looked at the floor and shook his head. "The Germans became harsh, more on people with French names, but everyone was unhappy. Most Alsatians, whatever their heritage, were happy to see the soldiers go."

Murphy looked up from his notes. "How do they all feel about the French soldiers here now?"

The man returned to his desk. "Most were enthusiastic when they arrived, and few people object to France's takeover, although there are many who would like to see us independent again. We have our own culture, different from either of the two countries. Whatever happens, we will make do."

"Can I take your photo?"

"Of course." He stood still and smiled while Murphy snapped a shot.

Outside, Murphy searched the street for a business that had a German name on it. He spotted a cleaners that did. After taking a picture of the front of the business, he went in and met the owner, a man who appeared to be in his late forties. His hair was short cropped, and he had a thin mustache above his lip. He wore a crisp starched shirt. "Do you speak English?"

The man nodded. "Yes."

"I'm an American. My name is George Murphy. I work for my government. Can you tell me how you find it now that the French have taken over?"

"Mr. Murphy, even those of us of German heritage realize things are better now than they were during the war. Also, the way things are for Germany now, it is safer with France. You know the British navy still blockades German ports. They will not allow any food in. It is not a problem here. Before the war we were happy with German rule, but we cannot go back to what was."

Back at his hotel room, he sat and analyzed what he had learned so far. The people he spoke to were consistent in their observations. Murphy's own general observations were more important. Even though French troops were here, the place did not have the feel of occupied territory. Everyone behaved free and easy, and the French soldiers who patrolled the streets fit in as well as local cops. There was no apparent friction. He looked at the camera. It was a Kodak Brownie Box. He put it in the bottom drawer of the dresser. Tomorrow he would try to see the rest of Strasbourg. *What will I learn in the museums?*

After dinner, Murphy stopped for a cognac at a café before heading back to the hotel. It had gotten cooler, and he was glad for his jacket. As he neared the corner, he saw an attractive woman coming the other way. She was well dressed in a coat with a fur collar and a sash at the waist. Over her long blond hair she wore a checkered hat with a brim. It occurred to him Fiona might dress that way if she were in Germany rather than France. As she approached Murphy, she smiled but, without warning, slapped him hard across the face and screamed. Several people ran over, including two French soldiers. The woman pointed at Murphy as she shouted, "This man, he grabbed me and dragged me toward the alley."

Murphy was flabbergasted. "What? I don't know what she's talking about."

The soldiers took hold of him, and one said, "You are coming with us." They brought Murphy to the police station on Rue de la Nuée-Bleue and placed him in a small room with a table and four chairs. "Stay here while we talk to the victim."

Over an hour and a half went by before they came back, still curt. "We cannot find the woman, either here or back where you assaulted her. You should tell us what you know if you do not want to end up in even more trouble!"

Near the back of Fiona's hotel where shops were located, she observed a perfumery. *Oh for a bottle of good French perfume, I should have brought some money from Ireland, but we had to get out of there too fast after the funeral. I may not have much. but enough to treat myself.* Inside the shop she selected a small bottle of Guerlain Mitsouko Extrait de Parfum, reached deep into the compartment at the bottom of her purse and paid for it.

As she was leaving the shop she heard a young woman plead in a German accent. "But I promised my mother I would send her back a bottle of French perfume."

The proprietress snarled at her. Tell her to rub herself with your German sauerkraut."

The girl cried, "I'm all she has left. My father and my brother, both killed in war. All we have is my job with our delegation. My mother used to live here. She speaks French. She did not want war."

The woman pursed her lips and squinted. "She got the war, but she will not get the perfume."

Fiona waited outside the shop. The young woman wept as she walked out. Fiona walked up to her and placed the bottle she had bought in the woman's hands. The woman had trouble speaking and reached into her own purse, but Fiona held up her hand, smiled, and walked away without a word.

She strolled along until her eyes caught something that made her gasp. There on the front page of the newspaper was George's face with the headline, "American Army Officer Arrested for Assaulting Another Woman." The byline was Henri Durand's. She bought a copy of the paper and raced back to her room. *What can I do? If this had happened in Paris, the police would already know it was a setup, but Strasbourg doesn't even have a working police force yet, only soldiers. Lieutenant Coderre gave me his card with a phone number on it.* She dialed it, identified herself and Coderre was placed on the line. "What can I do for you Mademoiselle McDermott?"

She held the receiver with unsteady hands. "Have you seen this morning's newspaper?"

"You mean the article about Lieutenant Murphy. I have."

"Can someone from your department contact the army authorities in Strasbourg and tell them about the history of false accusations against George? Otherwise they might believe this woman."

"I cannot do it on my own, but I can talk to Commissaire Trudeau about it."

She moved the phone to her other ear. "Please, Lieutenant Coderre, the army in Strasbourg knows nothing of the history of this."

After getting off the telephone with Lieutenant Coderre, Fiona set out for the Hôtel de Crillon. *I need to speak with someone in the American delegation. George's friends should be the most helpful.*

When she was shown in to see Richard Ambrose, he rose to meet her. "I guess you've seen the newspaper!"

She held her gloves in one hand and smacked the desk with them continuously. "I have. Is anything being done to contact the French authorities in Strasbourg?"

Richard sighed. "We have tried, but have run into a major roadblock."

She stopped swinging her gloves. "Why? What do you mean 'roadblock?'"

"Our delegation's major contact with the French Army was Général Moinier, the military governor of Paris. He was thoroughly familiar with all the bogus accusations, including those against George. He could have straightened things out for us."

Fiona lifted her hands. "Why can't he do it now?"

"He's died."

Fiona dropped her hands. "Oh, no!"

"General Harts is trying to contact Moinier's replacement, but it will take time. He is sure to have bigger problems right now."

❧

In Strasbourg a French army sergent addressed Murphy. "What is your name?"

Murphy was disheveled from sitting up all night, so he combed his fingers through his hair. "Lieutenant George Murphy, United States Army."

The sergent's chair, like the others in the room, had no arms. "And what are you doing here in Strasbourg?"

Murphy tried to sit up straight. "Preparing to report back to the American peace delegation about your progress in reclaiming Alsace and Lorraine."

The sergent scoffed. "Why would the Americans need their own report. We can tell them anything they need to know."

Murphy wrapped his arms back around the chair. "There isn't a diplomat in the world who will go into an international conference without dossiers prepared by his own delegation."

The plain table they were seated at had folding legs. The sergent rested his elbows so far forward his chin almost rested on it. "Why did you attack the woman last night?"

"I didn't."

He straightened. "Why did she say you did?"

"Probably because she was working for someone who wants to embarrass both France and the United States."

The sergent spread his hands in the air. "How could this incident embarrass France?"

Murphy stretched his legs. "If you contact the Préfecture de Police in Paris, Commissaire Trudeau can explain it to you. There has been an ongoing effort by parties unknown to drive a wedge between the French and the Americans, mostly by false accusations of crimes. I have been one of the favorite targets. Général Moinier is well aware of it. You can contact him also."

The sergent barked. "Why has this woman disappeared?"

Murphy inclined his head toward the sergent. "She was probably paid to accuse me and vanish before she could be questioned. Even if I were as vile as you seem to think, why would I attack a woman with so many people, including two of your soldiers, so near at hand?"

The sergent did not say another word but turned and left the room abruptly.

Murphy couldn't remember feeling this miserable. He had been more tired and dirty in the trenches, but his spirit was better then. How long had he been in this bare room? Was it fifteen hours already with nothing to eat? Why, when he finally thought he had developed the self-confidence he needed, did this happen? What would he tell Ambassador White?

He jumped when the door flew open and the sergent entered. "You probably don't think we soldiers are good at detective work, do you?"

"I don't know what to think. I'm a soldier but have been assigned more than my fair share of it."

The sergent rested his hands on the back of a chair. "We found your camera."

"If you searched my room it shouldn't have been too hard. It was in the bottom drawer of the dresser."

The sergent scoffed. "Not unless the dresser was under the bed, off the floor, tied to the springs with a wire."

"Under the bed? You can't be serious. Why would I hide it? All I was photographing were people and shops. Ambassador White gave me the camera for that purpose."

"That may be why he gave it to you, but you apparently had other ideas."

Murphy was almost yelling. "What? That's crazy."

"No, lieutenant what you did was crazy. Why did you take this photo?" He placed it on the table.

Murphy grabbed it and his eyes flew wide. It showed a battery of French 75 millimeter guns pointed at the bridge across the Rhine, which was visible in the background. "I never took this photo or anything like it. Why would I? I fought the Germans and was wounded by them."

"Monsieur, it is no secret that there is a growing movement in Germany to restart the war. It is also likely it would make Strasbourg its first target. Those guns would be critical to our defense, if that were to happen, a photo, showing their exact location would permit the Germans to pinpoint them with their own artillery."

"Why would I ever do a stupid thing like that to aid the enemy against an ally?"

The sergent had a half smile. "Perhaps for the twenty thousand German marks under your mattress."

Murphy's chest was over the table. "I've never even seen a German mark let alone possessed twenty thousand of them!"

CHAPTER XIX

FIONA WAS STARING at the floor in the Crillon, shaking, when Richard took her by the arm. "Let's have a coffee in the lobby."

She looked up at him. "Can we make it mineral water? I'm already jittery."

They sat at a coffee table. Richard had just placed the order when Captain Sanders approached their table. Fiona introduced the men. Sanders asked, "May I join you?"

Richard gestured at the empty chair. "Of course."

Sanders sat up straight looking at Fiona. "I tried to find you at your hotel. They told me you left to come here."

"I wanted to see if I could get help for George."

The captain looked down and drew in his breath. "He's going to need more than that."

Fiona looked up. "This is not the first time he's been falsely accused. He's gotten past such things before."

Sanders interlocked his fingers. "What do you know about the charges?"

"Only what I read in Durand's article."

"There's more."

Fiona sniffed. "What do you mean?"

"They found a picture on his camera of a French artillery position guarding the bridge over the Rhine. It show their relevant angles and distances."

This time it was Richard. "George would never do anything that stupid."

"They also found twenty thousand German marks under his mattress."

They were distracted as Stephen came hurrying over. "I just came from Ambassador White's office."

Richard held up his hand. "Are you going to tell us about the picture and the money too?"

Stephen froze. "How did you find out about that?"

"Captain Sanders here just told us."

He took the remaining seat on the sofa. "Ambassador White just heard from the French Foreign Office. Murphy's being held on espionage charges now."

Fiona jumped out of her chair. Started to totter and was helped to sit again. "George would never, never, never do that."

Sanders looked back at her. "Twenty thousand marks is a lot of motive."

Stephen jumped in. "In addition to trusting George, Ambassador White pointed out that he had been given both the mission and the camera just the night before. Even a crook couldn't have put together that highly complex a sellout in the short time involved!"

The sergent was staring at Murphy. "There's something else. When the soldiers went back to the scene of the incident, they did not find the woman who accused you but did find some of the witnesses. One of them had recognized her and knew where she lived. She was not happy when they paid a visit to her home. She is here now, at this station, in another room. We would like to talk to the two of you together."

Murphy's chest puffed. "A good idea!"

She was brought into the room. Unlike the night before she wore a plain brown dress. Her eyes widened when she saw Murphy. The sergent said, "Is this the man you were talking about?"

"Y... Yes."

The sergent asked, "What did he do?"

Her head dropped to her chest. "He grabbed me."

Murphy turned his chair toward her. "What part of your body did I grab?"

She pointed at her left arm. "Here."

"And which of my hands did I grab you with?"

She pointed to his right hand. "That one."

"And you say I dragged you toward an alley?"

She looked away but nodded her had repeatedly.

"Since the street was to my right, and the shops and alleys to my left, wouldn't I be dragging you away from the alley and toward the street, if I pulled your left arm with my right hand?"

She hesitated. "I don't know. Can't we forget this?"

"It's up to the sergent." Murphy took the photo of the mystery man from his pocket and showed it to her. "Do you recognize this man?"

As soon as she saw the photo she gasped. "Oh no!"

Murphy folded his hands. "Does that mean you do recognize him?"

"Look, he paid me to accuse you and go away. He said nothing would come of it if I was not there to testify. They would have to release you."

"How did he pay you?"

She sighed. "With German marks."

Murphy felt like his head was spinning. It took all his willpower to focus. *So the mystery man is in Strasbourg.* "Sergent, how many photos were on the film in my camera?"

The sergent shrugged. "Just three. This was the third."

"May I see the other two?"

He reached into an envelope. "Voila."

Murphy studied them and suddenly smiled. "Sergent, I took the first two photos late yesterday afternoon. You can verify that with the bookseller and the cleaner."

"We already have."

"You can also see in the photo of the front of the cleaners that the sunlight is coming from the west, as it would late in the day."

"Yes we can."

"Now, when you look at the photo of the French artillery, the sun is obviously in the east. Its glare distorts the picture slightly."

"What are you getting at?"

"This photo was obviously taken in the morning. Also since it was the third and last photo of the roll of film, it had to be taken after I took the first two, which means it had to be taken this morning when I was here in your custody!"

Fiona was at the Grand Hôtel seated in the lobby with Captain Sanders when Murphy entered the room and walked over to them. She jumped up and gave him a big hug. Sanders lowered his eyes.

Fiona squeezed Murphy's arms with both her hands. "I heard you had been released, but when did you get back to Paris?"

"Just a short while ago. I stopped at the Crillon to drop off my report and came straight here."

"George, this is Captain Ted Sanders of MI5. Ted, this is Lieutenant George Murphy."

They shook hands. Sanders said, "Glad to see they let you go."

Fiona and Sanders resumed their seats, and Fiona folded her hands on her knees. "How long did they hold you? How did you manage to get released?"

"They held me from right after dinner until after lunch the next day. The French soldiers were able to track the woman who accused me, even though she had conveniently disappeared. She admitted having been paid off to make the accusation. She recognized the photo of the mystery man as the one who retained her. Once it became clear that the photo of the guns was taken while I was already in custody, I was released." Murphy put his hand on Fiona's shoulder and looked at the captain. "I hope I'm not interrupting anything important here."

Sanders got up and snatched his briefcase. "No, Fiona and I were just chatting over a cup of tea. I have to leave anyway, and you two have some catching up to do."

Murphy watched him leave and turned back to Fiona. "I see you're on a first name basis with MI5 now."

"Are you jealous, George?"

"Should I be?"

She tilted her head to the side with a sly grin. "Of course not!"

❧

Murphy and Fiona strolled along Rue Scribe. As they turned left on Rue Auber they admired the marble pillars alongside the opera house. Fiona slid her arm inside his. "George, what possible motive could the mystery man have for this?"

"It's obvious to me the newspaper article didn't result from the incident. It was more the other way around. The incident was staged to facilitate the newspaper article. I wouldn't be surprised if the article were written beforehand."

Fiona turned and snickered at him. "Go on now!"

His pace slowed. "No, no, look at what happened with the phony American crime wave. We know the reports are false. The French police know the reports are false, but I bet a lot more people remember the newspaper articles than remember the follow-up."

Fiona stopped and turned to him. "Why didn't the article mention the photograph of the cannons? That would be bigger news."

Murphy held up a hand. "That concerned me too, but think of this. The mystery man knew what the woman was going to do with me in advance and was able to get the story back to his associates in Paris in time to get it published. But he did not know that he was going to find a camera in my hotel room. While he was able to use it to take the incriminating photo and plant it and the money back in my room, it was too late to get a story in the morning paper. He would have had to wait another day, and by then I had an ironclad alibi."

"Oh George, why would anyone go to all this trouble?"

"I've been thinking about that. Are they trying to point a finger back at the Germans? The mystery man paid the woman in German marks. Then he left marks in my room. My one contact with German intelligence insists it's not them, and Martine Joossens is absolutely convinced they're Bolsheviks, that the whole thing is a Russian ploy."

Fiona whispered in his ear. "Assuming she's right, where are they going with it?"

"We have to separate the phony crime wave from everything else that happened beginning with Angeline, whose real name was Natasha, asking Claude to introduce her to me." He took her arm. "Once we eliminate the crime wave we have: Angeline's deceptive approach to me, her appearing to be frightened by the mystery man, his being photographed following me, Angeline's murder in my apartment, your being shot at by Bennett, the mystery man's appearance at Angeline's funeral, your being assaulted by Ostomeyer, your being followed by Bennett, my being followed to Strasbourg by the mystery man and his paying a woman with German marks to falsely accuse me. Plus the photo."

She turned her head. "Not to mention someone killing the sniper in Ireland!"

He offered Fiona his hand. "We now know for sure Angeline was a Russian pretending to be Belgian. Bennett pretended to be English. Ostomeyer and the mystery man pretend to be German. Doesn't it make better sense if they were all working together, in which case they would all be Russian?"

Fiona slid her arm through his. "I see your point. It would be a strange coincidence indeed for four different people from three different countries to target the two of us, out of the blue and all at the same time. They have to be working together for the same country, and since the only one whose nationality we can be sure of now was Russian, they must all be Russian."

"I have an idea. The French police suggested conducting countersurveillance of me, not for my protection, but to see if it can lead them to whoever murdered Angeline, but following me hasn't produced anything since the photo of the mystery man. If he is associated with the people we know as Major Bennett and Herr Ostomeyer, if they're all part of the same conspiracy, maybe they can discover more by conducting countersurveillance of you."

Her head touched his shoulder. "It's worth a try if they will do it. When I first came here to Paris I would have objected to having law enforcement following me around. Now, since I'm likely to be followed anyway, I'd rather know who's doing it, and I'd prefer the French to the British!"

They jumped as a flashbulb went off in their faces—who should be holding the camera but Henri Durand. "How did you get released from jail in Strasbourg?"

Murphy resumed walking with Fiona but needed to give some answer. "The woman who accused me admitted she was paid off to do it."

Durand yelled back, "Who would pay her to do such a thing?"

"The same person who sent you the report of the incident before it even occurred."

Durand stopped in his tracks!

ꟹ

It wasn't until much later that the mystery man made it back to Paris. His first stop was at an apartment on Rue Greffulhe in the Eighth Arondisement. A woman answered his knock. "You're back. You have probably seen the newspaper article that was published, but why were you in Strasbourg at all?"

"I followed Murphy there and took the opportunity to add more confusion."

She snarled. "You're throwing a lot of marks around."

He smiled. "Don't worry. The Germans are printing them as fast as they can now, and we have comrades on the inside. Within a year they'll probably be worthless."

The woman glared. "Remember we need Murphy here, not in some prison."

"There was no way the case against him would stand up once the professional intelligence people from both countries became involved. I was just surprised that Murphy was able to shoot it down so fast himself, but it might still keep them focused on the Germans."

ꟹ

Fiona was to have dinner with Captain Ted Sanders. With everything that was happening, it didn't hurt to keep this line open. She also found she enjoyed his company. He picked her up in an official car he drove himself. She did not expect him to take her to a railroad station, the Gare de Lyon. Sanders parked the vehicle, and they entered the terminal. No sooner were they inside than they turned completely around in the opposite direction and went up a stairway. It seemed more like a church than a restaurant. The images were not religious, but the walls and vaulted ceiling were covered with elaborate murals and molding surrounding grand chandeliers. The tables backed up to cushioned banquettes finished in deep blue leather with dark wooden framing topped with brass rails and lamp posts. Fiona sat on one of the banquettes.

Sanders took a chair facing her and ordered a bottle of Bordeaux. "The renovation of this railroad station, including the restaurant was a major project at the turn of the century. The architect was Marius Toudoire, and the artwork here is outstanding."

Fiona tore her eyes off the ceiling. "I can see. This is the most majestic restaurant I have ever seen. But I must thank you for all your help."

Sanders unfolded his napkin. "I haven't done much at all."

"That's not true, Ted. You told me about the matching bullets and informed us about the photos and German marks."

"You would have learned about the latter from Stephen Brown within minutes anyway."

Fiona chuckled. "I don't know where it's leading to yet, but it's worth knowing, and don't worry I am being cautious. I didn't even engage in any politics while I was in Ireland."

"No, you didn't, but it didn't keep someone from

stalking you anyway." The waiter arrived with the wine, Sanders tasted it, nodded, and the waiter poured two glasses. Sanders set his on the table. "You stayed away from politics on that trip, but we both know you can't once this conference is over. As I've said before, I'm no politician, and there are a lot of people in Great Britain who favor home rule for Ireland. I think it's inevitable myself, but I am worried about the escalating violence on both sides. Some people avoid speaking out because they're afraid of all the parties. You don't have that option. You've made clear your position and broadcast it to the world."

"To the point where some people in Ireland avoid me, not to mention those trying to kill me."

The waiter arrived to take their order. Fiona ordered smoked salmon to start followed by filet of Turbot. Sanders started with foie gras and ordered Veal Foyot as his main course. He took a swig of his wine. "Don't get me wrong, I don't disagree with your goals, but I do worry about your personal safety. There is a plan to recruit unemployed war veterans from Great Britain, with no law enforcement experience, as auxiliaries to the Royal Irish Constabulary. If it happens, don't expect them to act like professional police officers. They won't."

Fiona swirled the wine in her glass. "Ted, my personal safety isn't on firm footing, no matter where I am."

Sanders hesitated. "This may be an inappropriate question, but how close are you to Lieutenant Murphy?"

"It's not inappropriate. We have a serious relationship, but I have limitations."

He swallowed. "The reason I bring it up is something

I never thought I'd say, but, if you went to America with him, those risks would surely disappear."

Fiona squeezed her shoulders together. "Ted, you're familiar with my history. You know I could never make an acceptable wife for him."

He was quick to interject, "Fiona, please don't sell yourself short. You're one of the most attractive and talented women in Paris, which is a difficult venue to compete in. Times are changing. We have just seen the collapse of the five biggest monarchies in the world, excluding our empire. Lots of women with your type of background have married and raised families and most of them didn't have your political and diplomatic status."

The waiter served their appetizers. Fiona used her fork to lay a slice of salmon on a corner of toast. She topped it with chopped onion and capers. "I do appreciate your concern, Ted, and George would certainly go along with what you suggest, but I can't. Now let's enjoy this fine food and not worry about tomorrow!"

CHAPTER XX

WHEN MURPHY RAISED the countersurveillance issue with Commissaire Trudeau the commissaire greeted it with enthusiasm. "A good idea. Whoever was following you was interested in damaging your reputation, not in hurting you physically. Also, as far as we have been able to determine, no one is following you now, other than us. Mademoiselle McDermott, on the other hand, has been shot at, assaulted in a car, and made the target of a now dead sniper. Two of those incidents happened within our jurisdiction. The approaches to her have been of a more violent nature, as was the one to Mademoiselle DuBois. You may be right that we will learn more by following Mademoiselle McDermott than by following you. Of course, it depends on the incidents being related, but that seems likely with the same gun being used in two incidents, one here and one in Ireland."

When Murphy arrived at the Hôtel de Crillon the next morning he was stunned to find Captain Sanders waiting to see him. They shook hands. *Why is he here? What is he up to?* Still Murphy had to be cordial. "What can I do for you?"

"I wanted to discuss the situation regarding Fiona McDermott."

Murphy stood stone still. "What situation?

Sanders's chin jutted forward. "Look here, she has been followed, molested and shot at here in Paris. She was also nearly assassinated in Ireland, only to be saved by the same person who shot at her here. If that doesn't add up to a situation, I don't know what does."

Murphy accepted the folder of invoices Madame Hardy held out to him and brought Sanders to his desk where they both sat. "What does MI5 have to do with it?"

Sanders placed his hand on the desk. "The man who did most of those things impersonated an MI5 officer to you, a member of the staff of a foreign diplomatic delegation. That alone is all the jurisdiction I need. In addition, Fiona is still a British subject, even if the thought does not please her."

Murphy rubbed his wounded arm. "Are you sure there's not a personal reason behind this?"

Sanders braced his shoulders. "Does it matter if there is?"

Murphy shrugged. *How would Fiona feel, if she knew about this encounter?* "Probably not, but where do you want to take this?"

"Do you have any idea who is doing this?"

Should I tell him? He's going to find out anyway. He repeated for Sanders what Martine had told him and showed him the school photograph. As expected, the captain almost fell out of his chair. He composed himself. "Does anyone know what the objective of their operation is?"

"I have lots of ideas, but none I can support with real evidence. I can't even figure out who the real target is, Fiona or me." Murphy dumped the invoices onto the growing stack of those he had not yet reviewed. "Mr. O'Kelly told me about the Soviet activity in Ireland, something I was unaware of. He also explained their antipathy toward Fiona, but that wouldn't explain why they set Angeline, Natasha, on me before I even met Fiona." He turned his full attention back to Sanders. "I'm not important enough to have a negative impact on the American delegation. What do you think? You're the counterintelligence officer. I'm just a document translator given other occasional projects."

Sanders glanced around the room. "I wanted to have someone follow Fiona, not to impede her, but to identify the culprits. My superiors wouldn't go for it, in any event. Impersonating an MI5 officer isn't a serious enough offense to justify that big a commitment of resources. Even with this new information we can't provide security for every British subject in France or give her priority simply because she works for the provisional Irish government which we don't recognize."

Murphy froze. *What is this man up to? Is this dramatic show of concern simply a charade to justify a crackdown on Fiona and on the Irish delegation in general?* "You would have her followed?"

"Solely for her own safety."

Murphy chose not to mention his own plan to have her followed by the French police. "And what if this British agent following her observed her doing something that violated British law? Remember she sincerely believes the United Kingdom has no jurisdiction over her, that she's a citizen of the Republic of Ireland and obedient to its laws only."

Sanders lowered his voice. "Lieutenant Murphy, it may surprise you, but I'm not sure she isn't right. It may well be, within a few years, even our government will agree, but that's not the point. The point is her safety."

"She would not see it that way."

"No, no she wouldn't. You're right, but there's no sense arguing about it anyway, since my superiors won't allow it. I still feel something more must be done, but thank you for sharing the information obtained from the Belgian woman." He stood up.

Murphy stood up with him. "Captain Sanders, I'm not insensitive to what you're saying, but I know Fiona will not go along with any of it. The only truly effective way to protect an individual like Fiona is to catch the people after her. They do not hesitate to use violence. As to me, they seem more interested in damaging my reputation."

"And they're succeeding!" Sanders walked away.

ᔓ

Murphy brought the photograph he received from Martine to his meeting with General Harts. "I thought you would want to see this, sir. I don't know where to go from here. I realize it's not my job to be conducting an investigation, but things I can't ignore keep happening to me and to Fiona McDermott."

Harts took the picture. "No you can't ignore them. What's more, even we seem to get more valuable information via you than from any of our other sources. Martine Joossens came to you, not to our intelligence people, and let's not forget they got the photograph of the mystery man by following you."

Murphy put his hands on his thighs. "It's now clear, at least as far as Fiona's and my problems go, we are not dealing with the British or with the Germans. What we are faced with are deadly Russian assassins who know who we are and where we are, while we know next to nothing about them. The pattern of events worries me even more."

Harts folded his hands. "How so?"

Murphy held up a hand. "Two days after I first meet Angeline, she gets murdered in my apartment." He looked down. "Two days after I take Fiona to lunch at the Crillon this Bennett comes up to me, denounces my actions and makes threats against her. Then what he threatens happens. I don't think it's a coincidence. That's why I wanted to talk with you, sir."

The general returned the picture. "Lieutenant, the only thing I can tell you is to keep your ears and your eyes open. Public attacks like what happened to Miss McDermott on the Champs-Élysées cannot be their ultimate goal, nor can the accusations against you. The Soviets resented her well before you came along, but they might use you as a smokescreen. Much of that was already in place because of what happened with Miss DuBois. Miss McDermott knows enough now not to go in a car with anyone she doesn't know well, and it was wise moving you into the Hôtel Continental to avoid your being confronted in an outlying private residence. The one thing we want to avoid is for either of the two of you to be accosted in private!"

ශ

Murphy was to pick up Fiona for dinner at eight o'clock. In her room, she retouched her makeup, adjusted her hat and opened the door to depart. She stepped out and stopped cold! Stuck on the outside of her door was a dead bird, a pretty blue oiseau staked onto the wood by a hatpin through its throat. Fiona put her hand to her mouth before she heard, "Good evening, Miss McDermott, you stupid Catholic bitch, you expected me to say 'Fr*ä*ulein!' Still think we're German?"

She looked at him. Herr Ostomeyer grinned back. "You have no idea who we are, but we know who you are and where you are! Don't count too much on that American… Irish-American, Catholic, boyfriend of yours, a boy scout way over his head." He turned and raced to the stairway.

Fiona slammed the door shut and rushed to the elevator. It couldn't come quickly enough. She told the operator, "Please, to the lobby, right away. It's an emergency."

She ran out and spotted Murphy who took her by the shoulders. "What is it?"

"Herr Ostomeyer. He nailed a dead bird to my door, with a hatpin no less! Then sped down the stairs." She grabbed Murphy's forearms and put her head on his shoulder.

Murphy broke away, ran to the stairwell, looked around, came back and squeezed her to him. "He obviously planned his escape ahead of time. Searching for him is of no use! You need a brandy."

She choked. "Make it a big one."

Murphy placed the order before calling the préfecture to let them know. "They will want to examine the evidence themselves."

By the time he returned Fiona had half finished her drink. He sat on the chair facing the couch and took a swig of his. "They're coming right over."

"They better! George, Ostomeyer's now playing anti-Catholic Irish militia, even went on to ridicule you as a boy scout, and Catholic yourself."

"Oh my God, Fiona, even more scary!"

"No, George… As Martine says, they're undoubtedly Russian, And, George, while some of your social skills may be lacking. In real danger, I would trust you, more than any other person alive."

It didn't take long for the police to arrive. George and Fiona hadn't finished their drinks when Lieutenant Coderre appeared with a uniformed officer. After some discussion the officers went up the stairs to Fiona's room. Fifteen minutes later they came back. The uniformed officer was carrying a bag. They took a brief statement and left.

Fiona put her hand on Murphy's shoulder. "I don't feel like eating."

He rubbed her hand. "Let's just sit here."

She reached for her glass. "George, I have something to tell you."

Murphy took a sip from his. "What's that?"

She set her glass back on the table. "You may have to rethink the way you feel about Captain Sanders. He took me to dinner and told me the only safe thing I can do now is to move to America with you."

Murphy's eyes widened. "Did he offer to take you someplace himself first?"

She wiggled and smiled. "He did not, but who knows what he would do, if he thought he had an opening."

Murphy rested back against his chair. "Where did he tell you this?"

"At the restaurant in the Gare de Lyon."

"That's an extravagant setting for telling a woman she should go away with another man, if that was what he originally intended."

"It was one of the most gorgeous settings I have ever seen. I did feel flattered."

"I better get you there myself." He moved to sit next to her on the couch and slid his glass around the table. "Fiona, forget what he told you and forget what I told you. Just think about what happened tonight. How much of this can you take?"

"George, both of you are right about the risks I am facing. I know. He is not my love. You are, but I cannot back off. You, of all people, should realize that."

"I do, but here and now your political activities are not the cause of the risk. I don't know what is, but let's look at what has happened. Angeline had nothing whatsoever to do with Ireland. The mystery man followed me to Brussels after she was dead. If she was a Bolshevik agent, why was she killed? If the mystery man's pursuit of her was genuine, why did she help establish his false identity? Remember she claimed to have seen him in Belgium at a time we now know she was in Russia. What further interest could he have in me, if she was the real target? But Sanders is right.

Whoever is after you would probably give up if we were both in the United States. Have you given it any thought?"

Fiona looked up. "George, I have thought about it, but it's a pipe dream, like, 'Wouldn't it be nice if?,' but then it runs up against the real world. I can't desert Ireland now. I don't know which is worse, British subjugation or Bolshevik infiltration!"

⁂

Two days later, as Fiona walked through the lobby of the Grand Hôtel, Sean O'Kelly called to her to join him. "Do you have a minute to talk?"

"I'm free right now. George Murphy is taking me to dinner tonight, so I'll need to get ready in a little while."

He smiled. "It sounds like you two are quite close."

Her shoulders sagged. "We are close, but I can't see it lasting. Can you?"

"I can, or rather, I could, but for some recent developments."

Her lips stiffened. "What recent developments?"

"Collins wants you back in Ireland."

Her face froze. "Why?"

"He feels it's too dangerous for you here now. You've been attacked twice and otherwise bullied. There have been no arrests, so the culprits are still out there."

"And if the British or northern Irish are behind it, I'll be safer here than in Ireland."

O'Kelly lowered his head. "That's a big 'if,' Fiona. Bennett claimed he was British, but he also claimed he was

MI5. We know the latter part wasn't true. Why should we believe anything he says?"

Fiona sat on the couch. "Even if the people after me here are not British, there's no question what the sniper they killed in Ireland was, and there are others like him there."

He grimaced back at her.

"Can I contact Michael myself?"

O'Kelly dropped his head. "It would be difficult and clumsy, considering our timespan. The only quick way to contact him is by telegram, and that would be too risky. You'll have to make your pitch to Collins in person. Here's what we can do. Go to your dinner with George Murphy tonight. Tomorrow one of our security people will ride with you on the train to Cherbourg, where he will put you on the ferry to Dublin. Once you get there you can work your charms on Michael Collins, and maybe come back."

CHAPTER XXI

MURPHY GOT TO the lobby of the Grand Hôtel at seven twenty, less than two minutes before Fiona stepped off the elevator. "So, you are taking me to Rue Edouard VII. It's not a long walk."

"I planned it that way."

They were shown to a table next to a window looking out on the square. The long purple drapes touched the rich hardwood floor.

"What would you like to drink, Fiona?"

She touched his hand. "You pick something."

As the waiter placed menus in front of them, Murphy ordered a bottle of Chardonnay. He raised his eyes from the menu. "The seafood here is supposed to be good. I'm thinking of trying the Spaghettis aux fruits de mer."

"I will have whatever you're having."

Murphy ordered it for both of them with Britannia Oysters to start. Fiona took a sip of her wine. "This may be our last meal together."

Murphy almost knocked his glass over. "What? Why? Is something wrong?"

She sighed. "I'm being recalled to Ireland."

"How did this happen?"

"Michael Collins thinks I'm going to get killed if I stay here."

Murphy stared at his wine glass for a few seconds. "I'm afraid he may be right, but will you be any safer in Ireland?"

"If the British want to kill me, it would be easier for them to do in Ireland, but, if I were there, instead of here, they might have no motive to do so. My value to the cause there will be minimal. The bad publicity from my murder would hurt them worse than any service I could perform back home, and we now know the real problem here is the Bolsheviks."

Murphy's body was frozen. "But the Bolsheviks followed you to Ireland too."

"But look at what they did there, kept one of my usual enemies from killing me!"

Murphy hung his head.

Fiona placed her wine glass back. "George, I just don't know. I am being escorted to Cherbourg to board the ferry to Dublin. That much I cannot change. All I can hope is once I get to speak to Collins in person, I can convince him it is better for me to be here."

"I sure hope you succeed."

She edged close to him and whispered, "Do you promise to think of me every day?"

"You've become Paris for me. Without you it won't mean much."

She giggled. "You certainly have an overblown sense of

my importance if you believe my presence or absence will have any measurable effect on the ambience of this ancient and celebrated city."

Murphy lowered his eyes. "I can't talk about the ambience of the whole city, only about the way I experience it."

Fiona murmured, "George, they're not giving me any choice."

He sat up. "There are still some choices I can make, and if you don't come back, you're going to see me back there again."

She whimpered. "You'll find me waiting for you!"

⁂

Murphy was at the Continental Hôtel when he spotted Congressman Hamill seated at a table in the lobby speaking with two other men. He approached the congressman. "Please excuse me for interrupting, but I don't know if you are aware Fiona McDermott is being sent back to Ireland today."

Hamill turned to him. "I did hear of it, George. Sean O'Kelly told me yesterday. Everyone will miss her. She lit up the room wherever she went, and I'm not sure she'll be any safer in Ireland than she would be here, but I want to introduce you to these gentlemen. This is Mr. Hryhorii Sydornko, chief of the Ukrainian delegation, and this is Mr. Vladimir Timoshenko, also of the delegation. Gentlemen, this is Lieutenant George Murphy of the American delegation." They exchanged greetings. Hamill gestured at an empty chair. "Why don't you join us, George? These gentlemen have an interesting proposal."

Murphy took the seat. *I hope I can get the congressman alone to talk about Fiona.*

Timoshenko turned to Murphy. "These times have been difficult for the Ukraine. To begin with, we were not regarded as a country at all but as a part of the Russian Empire even though we had a different language, religion, and culture."

Murphy rested his elbows on the arms of the chair. "I understand your church is still in communion with the pope, even though your practices are more similar to the orthodox."

"That is correct. Our Masses are said in Ukrainian rather than in Latin, and our priests may marry, but we still acknowledge the pope as the head of the Catholic Church, of which we are a part."

Murphy nodded. "The Ukraine is in a critical location."

"We were caught between the Russians on one side and the Austro-Hungarians on the other. Our homes became their battlefield. Things became even worse after the Russian Revolution as the Russians were split into different factions, each one of them taking revenge on us Ukrainians, and now they don't want us to be heard here, but we must be heard, or this will never stop."

Murphy spread his hands. "What is being done now?"

Hamill lifted his head. "So far we have not made much progress, but things might change now. These gentlemen have a proposal that might work. Mr. Timoshenko…"

Timoshenko faced the table. "Being seated at the conference becomes less and less important every day. Only the big four can get anything done, and France is one of the big four. We believe we can get France to support our claim to our own nation."

Murphy shifted his weight. "How do you propose to do it?"

"Russia owes France much money for loans made as part of alliance with czarist government. Chances the Soviets will repay it do not exist. We offer to pay France our share of the debt if we become independent state."

"Do you have the money to do it?"

"No, we have something much better."

Murphy sat up straight. "Which is?"

Timoshenko smiled. "Wheat, something the French have great need of now with their own farm fields turned into trenches!"

Murphy rubbed his lips together. "I have to admit, it is a remarkable plan. I hope you succeed."

"Now it is best hope."

Murphy sat back. "Is this plan confidential?"

"Not at all. We are issuing a press release about it."

As they got up Murphy was still in a haze. *Fiona is gone. I didn't get the chance to discuss it with Hamill. Did she mean it when she said she'd be waiting for me? She pretends to be enamored of everything but why would she encourage me to come if it's not what she wanted? If she didn't want me to come, she would certainly make sure I understood.*

The day after Fiona arrived in Dublin she was dining in a pub with her new roommate, Brigid O'Hanlon. She scanned the room. It was all there: the heavy framed mirrors emblazoned with the names of beers and ales, the brass rails on the dark wood paneling, the crystal lights hanging from the ceiling, even a stag's head on the wall over the bar. The aroma of beer penetrated the tobacco smoke. She felt at home here as she enjoyed both the Guinness and the bangers and mash. "Since I have been in Paris so much has happened here. I know the details of the Declaration of Independence, but what has life been like?"

Brigid placed her glass down in front of her. "Ireland is becoming a war zone. There may not be any pitched battles between armies, but ambushes are common. The British are responding with raids on people's homes and farms. Don't be surprised if we get our apartment door broken open some night by police claiming to be investigating crimes. The fact we work for a government they don't recognize may well be enough."

"So the war to end all wars did not do it?"

Brigid sighed. "Not in Ireland, but what about Paris? Are the clothes there as nifty as everyone says?"

Fiona smiled. "They are that and more."

Brigid raised her head and smiled. "I read in the newspaper you were clothes shopping when you were shot."

Fiona held up her hand. "I wasn't really shot, Brigid. The bullet missed me and broke the shop window. I was only cut by shattered glass."

"Some newspapers said your gentleman friend was behind it."

Fiona squared her shoulders. "He certainly was not. The man who did the shooting made some threats to George about someone wanting to harm me, and he passed them on to the authorities."

Brigid slid forward. "And you're stepping out with an American army officer!"

Fiona took a deep breath. "I was, but I'm not in Paris anymore."

"How do you feel about him? Will he come here to see you?"

Fiona lifted her glass. "He said he would, and I encouraged him. I hope it wasn't a mistake."

Brigid glared at her. "How could it be that now?"

"Brigid, it's too late for me to have that kind of life. People admire my political skills, but my personal reputation is a mess. I need to dedicate myself to the cause and nothing else. Unfortunately, my emotions are no longer cooperating with my plan."

Brigid lowered her voice and moved closer. "Does George know about your… reputation?"

Fiona nodded. "He does, I made sure to tell him myself."

"And did it upset him?"

"Not the slightest."

Brigid shook her head. "Then don't be a fool and give up. Do what your heart wants!"

❧

The next morning Fiona accompanied Brigid to work at the provisional government headquarters. As they entered the steno room the click-click of multiple typewriters stopped instantly. A woman's voice rang out. "What is this now? What are you staring at? Did you expect her to have two heads? Get back to work." Brigid introduced Fiona to her. The woman was the chief stenographer and about fifty years old. She wore a long skirt with a white blouse and looked Fiona up and down. "Can you type or take shorthand?"

Fiona shook her head. "I cannot do either."

"You will have to learn. We don't have any need here for your… usual talents." The woman shuffled the papers into a stack. "For now you can brew a pot of tea."

When it became time for lunch, Fiona went for a stroll. She had a large breakfast and wasn't hungry. She turned from Great Denmark Street onto Great George's Street, walking past rows of fine brick townhouses with brightly painted doors of assorted colors. All of the homes were equipped with wrought iron railings and flowerboxes. As much as she loved working for the provisional government, her present situation was not rewarding. In Paris everyone took her seriously. She didn't mind making tea, but there were more important things she could do.

As she turned onto Parnell Street, shops and pubs replaced the homes. There was also traffic, both automobile and horse drawn. People were walking on the sidewalk. As she strolled along she noticed a motorcycle, with a sidecar, coming in the opposite direction. There was a man in the sidecar. As it passed she felt something whish behind her before she heard the gunshot. A man on her right screamed and fell!

CHAPTER XXII

THREE DAYS LATER Murphy was at work at the Hôtel de Crillon. The others had already left for lunch, but he was still busy, so busy he didn't know she was there until a hand squeezed him softly on the shoulder. As he turned and looked up he heard her say, "I hoped to catch you in time."

He grasped the desk as he lurched to his feet knocking papers to the floor. "Fiona, You're here, not in Ireland. What did you tell Michael Collins to get back so fast."

"I will tell you about it, but let's go someplace. It's too nice a day to be shut in."

"The Champs-Élysées Garden is close."

They found a bench. Fiona took off her hat and ran her fingers through her hair. "As it turns out, I have our foes to thank for getting me back here."

Murphy put his arm on the back of the bench, behind her shoulder. "What? How so?"

"I was shot at again. This time I wasn't hurt." She told him what had occurred. "A man next to me took the bullet in his shoulder." She crossed her arms in front of her chest and rubbed her hands up and down her arms.

Murphy pulled his hand back and turned his head to see her better. "What happened? What did you do?"

"At the scene I didn't do anything. No one paid any attention to me. Everyone was focused on the wounded man. They didn't even take my name."

He put his hand on the back of her neck. "So now you're here?"

"When I got back to the office, I demanded to speak to Michael immediately. He was gracious about seeing me, and was shocked at what I told him. He agreed I was the real target but thought it best if we kept that quiet."

"So he decided to send you back?"

Fiona patted her hair in place. "His first suggestion was to assign me bodyguards, but it would be a big drain on our limited resources to protect a less than competent stenographer."

"So?"

Fiona put her hat back on, sliding it over her hair. "I told him the only answer was to send me back here. He pointed out it might be exactly what the shooter wanted. Why else would he miss at that range? I pointed out the sidecar he was riding in was attached to a motorcycle that had to take off at a high speed. More importantly, whatever he wanted, it was still our best course of action. If both Paris and Dublin present me with the same risk, am I not better off where I can be the most effective? So here I am!"

ꟹ

When he returned to his office Murphy was surprised to find Count Orlofsky waiting to see him. He extended his hand. "Please have a seat. How can I help you?"

The count sat. "It has come to my attention, from sources of my own, that you have recently learned the woman you were accused of murdering was not a Belgian named Angeline, as she claimed, but a Russian named Natasha Volkov?"

"Yes."

"I knew her parents. They were loyal to the czar, but she was Bolshevik!"

"Yes."

"And not only was she Bolshevik, she was a known Bolshevik agent?"

"Yes."

"You now know of the Soviet attempt to infiltrate the Irish home rule movement?"

"I do."

"You are also aware of their contempt for the bourgeoisie, especially for landowners like Miss McDermott, and that they resent her high standing with Irish Republicans?"

Murphy sniffed. "I've seen some of that firsthand."

Orlofsky sat back. "But why did Angeline made contact with you before you even met Miss McDermott."

"That one is still a mystery."

"I can help you with it. Their first scheme had nothing to do with Miss McDermott."

Murphy shook his head. "What was it then?"

Orlofsky leaned forward. "The Soviets have always been opposed to the Ukraine being recognized as a separate nation."

"I know."

"Well *they* knew that Congressman Hamill was your mentor, that he got you your job with the American delegation and that he's counsel to the Ukrainian one."

"So?"

"Their plan was to have you introduce her to Hamill and to use him as her entrée to the Ukrainian delegation. The talk about President Wilson was just a ruse."

Murphy pressed his lips together before speaking. "We already realized the Wilson thing was a ploy but have no idea of her real motive!"

Orlofsky settled a little but glared back. "The plan was to accuse a senior Ukrainian diplomat of sexual impropriety."

Murphy stiffened. "Would she do that?"

"Of course she would. That was what she did, but she didn't know the plan called for her to be murdered in your apartment so that you could be accused of killing her as a cover up."

"Wow! Oh my God!"

"She was not a member of the team that was conducting this operation. Her usual comrades were more accustomed to scams and blackmails than bloodshed. When they learned the team they leant her to was planning her death, her real team leader tried to pull her out. This prompted the killers to move the murder forward to frame you, but even that didn't work."

Murphy opened his hands. "Okay… okay, of this is terrifying, but I need to know is what are they doing now. What is going on?"

Orlofsky held up his fingers. "Your involvement with Miss McDermott was luck for them. Now they see opening to hit two bears with one spear. They can kill her and pass the blame off on you, and so avoid the consequences." The count waved his hand. "Lieutenant, you have to be extremely careful, now more than ever before. The people you are dealing with are utterly lethal, as you have already seen. Your relationship with Miss McDermott has given them another opening at you even more precarious than what it was with Natasha, Angeline. They always wanted to block recognition of the Ukraine, but Miss McDermott is big prize on her own."

He sat back in the chair. "So Fiona is taking Angeline's place as their path to me?"

Orlofsky threw his hands in the air. "Lieutenant, yes, that much is right, but that's not what this is all about. Right now it's about Fiona. She is much bigger target than you. With her gone the Bolsheviks think they would have real opening at the trade unions."

Murphy nodded. "I get it."

Wherever the Bolsheviks' plan to kill Miss McDermott, it will not be a public place where there will be witnesses who can clear you."

Murphy fidgeted. "I've already been told that."

"There's something you may not have been told." Orlofsky paused. "The private place they choose will most likely be in the Hôtel Continental. Your chamber is there, Hamill's chamber is there, and it is the headquarters of the Ukrainian delegation. You must make sure Miss McDermott stays away from Hôtel Continental and most of all from your room there until this can be cleared up."

Murphy planted his elbows on the desk. "Why should all of this concern you?"

The count's back was ramrod straight. "Lieutenant Murphy, I still consider myself to be an officer of the czar. God rest his soul. Those fiends slaughtered, not just him, but his wife, his four daughters and his son as well. The horror of it will never leave me. I knew every one of them personally. I will do anything in my power to keep those savage beasts from doing the same thing to anyone else!"

◆

Fiona arranged for Ted Sanders to meet her at the Grand Hôtel at three o'clock. She was not about to take the Metro to the Majestic after the last time. As she entered the lobby, he stood up from his chair. "Good afternoon, Fiona, your message caught me by surprise. Would you like some tea?" They sat and he placed the order. "What can I do for you?"

She took off her gloves and set them with her purse. "Ted, I know how good your sources are, so tell me what you know about what happened in Dublin."

He took a breath. "The police there were slow to pick up on your involvement. Once they realized what it was really about, the top echelon came in, and we were informed. Before you ask, it was a different gun, not the one used in the two previous incidents, but that doesn't mean it wasn't engineered by the same people."

Fiona shook her head. "Your government may not want me here, but it's obvious, even to me, that this is something else entirely. George and his Belgian contact think it's the Bolsheviks. I have reason to believe they're right, but they've never gone this far before with us. Their only successful inroads have been to the trade unions. We've given them nothing but a cold shoulder. Our concept of home rule does not translate to their desire for class warfare."

He looked across at her. "Most of your leadership comes from business or professional backgrounds and have no interest in Marxism. As you pointed out, however, the soviets have had some success with the working class in Ireland. I can easily see them trying to drive a wedge between you and the unions so that they can take over the home rule movement."

"How would killing me be of any benefit to them?"

He looked down. "You have to understand whom you're dealing with. In June of last year the Bolsheviks lost most of their country's territory. Leon Trotsky increased the size of the Red Army from three hundred thousand to one million and introduced what he calls political commissars. Since most of his officers were formerly loyal to the czar, their orders are no longer binding unless co-signed by a commissar, a devoted communist. Trotsky has said an army cannot be built without reprisals. He is now using what is known as Red Terror to eliminate the bourgeoisie as a class. Lenin is so upset with Trotsky's tactics he is trying, so far unsuccessfully, to get him removed as leader of the Red Army. I don't know which Bolshevik faction is after you, but its tactics look like Trotsky's."

She lifted her head. "What do you think of it?"

Sanders stretched the back of the sofa. "Fiona, even though our government opposes your official position, please remember what I told you the first time we met. I'm not a politician. My job is to avoid damage and, while you are here, that includes harm to you. From a personal standpoint also, I don't want to see you get hurt."

"Why?"

"I realize what a fine, dedicated person you are."

Fiona crinkled her eyes. "Ted, you're well aware my background is not all fine and dandy."

Sanders lowered his face. "I also know the pressure you were under at the time. The way you have conducted yourself since says much more about your character."

Fiona clenched her teeth. "The way I conduct myself now may be the result of my having nothing else to live for but Ireland."

"Please don't think that way. You are too exceptional a woman. As far as your safety, not only do we want you to stay safe, but so do the French police. The international community would not take it well if something else happened to you. You would not get the same support from the police in Ireland."

The tea arrived and Fiona accepted a cup. "I didn't even wait around for them, but the question still remains: Who doesn't want me in Ireland and why?"

Sanders put his cup on the table. "Things are going to get worse there. If this plan to recruit auxiliary constables from among unemployed war veterans takes hold, things are going to deteriorate quickly."

"But somebody wants me here, not there. What is the reason? Which is more important to them, that I be in Paris or that I not be in Dublin?"

Four people were gathered in a room in the Eighth Arondisement. Murphy knew them, so far, only as Herr Ostomeyer, whom he had never seen, Major Bennett and the mystery man whom he had and a short woman. They were not enjoying their meal. They didn't care about their meal. The mystery man pounded his fist on the table. "Now, now, now, they're both in Paris. Who knows when one or the other will leave again."

Major Bennett jumped to his feet. "If I did not eliminate the damn sniper before he got to the bitch in Ireland, where would we be now? Then she gets sent back to Ireland, and I have to find some low life there with a motorcycle and trust he can shoot and miss her. How many times can we get away with this?"

The short woman stood and surveyed the others. "Nothing will be accomplished by hysterics. Things are more critical now than they were with our phony Belgian girl. That was a small potato compared to what has happened since. We have been lucky. What were the chances that the same American officer we used in that scheme would become involved with a beautiful and prominent, bourgeois, anti-Bolshevik Irish Republican? We can't afford to make the same mistakes we made with the first one, but her team was onto us. We had to strike before they pulled her out, but look what that did. We couldn't nail either Murphy or the Ukrainians. We can't be rushed like that again with an even bigger target!"

Murphy was waiting in the café when Claude arrived and took a seat. "Mon ami, I was missing our conversations, but you had a lot on your hands."

Murphy had trouble turning his chair to face Claude as the man sitting behind him had his chair so close it was pressing against his. He wanted to tell Claude about Martine's revelation but didn't want anyone else overhearing. Fortunately, the man behind him chose this moment to stand and swagger to the door in his elegant gray suit. After noting the man was thin and appeared to be in his fifties, Murphy shifted his chair to a more comfortable position and proceeded to fill Claude in.

CHAPTER XXIII

BACK IN THE Eighth Arondisement, some way to the north, the short Russian woman was again meeting with her underlings. "Now is the time. We are ready. I will make the call to the McDermott girl, meet her in the lobby and escort her to the room. Konstantin," she said to Ostomeyer, "you will be waiting there for us to arrive. Have you tried your key on the door?"

"Yes, the wax impression I was able to make from Murphy's in the café produced a good duplicate. I checked the room for weapons but did not find any."

"Murphy and McDermott are both in Paris, so that won't be a problem, but we don't want anything going wrong like before." She turned to the man who called himself Major Bennett. "Boris, you have to make sure Murphy does not arrive back at the hotel early. If he leaves his office before the usual time, make sure he sees and recognizes you, then lead him on a wild goose chase in the opposite direction from the hotel. Go through Metro stations, run across the street against the light, do anything you can to stay ahead of him. Is that clear?"

He dropped his head. "Yes, it is."

To the mystery man, she said, "Ivan, you will be waiting by the lobby phone. When Murphy enters, ring the room once and hang up. Konstantin, you're our weapon person. What do you have this time?"

"What I've got now is good, more than good. It's a United States Army 1918 model fighting knife, not easy for anyone other than an American soldier to get, but I have my ways. It will point the finger at Murphy far more than a readily available bayonet would. Also, there are brass knuckles on the handle, so we can mess up our little honey before cutting her throat. I will make her sorry she stuck me in the neck. It will stir up more bitterness toward Murphy and his Ukrainian associates when everyone thinks he did it."

"Good, good. When you get Murphy in the room, make sure he does not have a gun on him. And remember, he can't have an alibi if he's in the room when the killing takes place. She must still be alive when he arrives."

After being shown into General Harts's office the next morning Murphy explained what Count Orlofsky had told him. The general stood up, looked at the map on the wall and turned back. "None of this is surprising, lieutenant. Yes, the Bolsheviks are trying to force their way into Ireland, and everywhere else. In Ireland, though, they've actually seized facilities and held them against the police, but they're not getting any support from the provisional government leadership in which Miss McDermott is a prominent figure. Of course they would want to get rid of her without getting blamed for it. Your czarist contact may be right. Their current plan would dovetail with the original one to make it look like you murdered Miss DuBois to cover up a sexual impropriety by a Ukrainian delegate. When they killed Angeline DuBois they had no idea you would later become involved with Fiona McDermott. They probably couldn't believe their luck when you did. Now they will attempt to bring about her death to advance both their plans. I agree with what the count said, that their scheme needs to be carried out in the headquarters hotel of the Ukrainian delegation. You must make sure Miss McDermott stays away from there."

Murphy sat up. "I will, sir. I'm having dinner with her tonight. I am going to pick her up at the Grand Hôtel and eat near there. We'll stay far away from the Continental."

"Make sure she understands the risk involved, even if it alarms her."

Murphy glanced back at him. "If there's one thing you don't have to worry about with Fiona, it's her becoming unduly alarmed. The real worry is her not being alarmed enough!"

Captain Ted Sanders was on his way to see Murphy. Somebody had to get Fiona out of Europe fast. France was not safe for her, nor were Britain or Ireland, and anything to the east would be a death trap. She might as well walk into the

Kremlin. He would take her to Australia or New Zealand if she would go with him but there was no chance of that happening. He had to convince Murphy to bring her to America or, more realistically, get him to convince Fiona to go. Someone had to get her to understand this was not the usual haphazard threats she was used to from Ireland. This was to be a cold-blooded and calculated liquidation by professionals so skilled that they were able to sneak up on and kill her would-be assassin in Ireland. They could slip up, like they did with the DuBois woman, but even that would not save Fiona any more than it did Angeline.

As he walked, he turned onto Rue de la Bienfaisance. What if she would go to Australia with him? His family would be furious. What would bother them more, that she was an Irish Republican or that she was of ill repute? Australia would be a good place to take her. There were lots of Irish there, and their penal colony history made them more forgiving of people's pasts. He looked ahead. *Who is that tall man? Could it be? It is. It's the man Fiona pointed out from the Hôtel Majestic, the one who called himself Major Bennett.*

Sergent Paul Cabal of the French police was waiting outside the Grand Hôtel. As part of the countersurveillance he had tailed Fiona there from her after lunch meeting. She had not been followed by anyone and was escorted by a provisional Irish delegation security man. Cabal was instructed not to go inside, but to observe what happened outside. He leaned against a lamppost. *I wish there were a bench to sit on. This could take a while.* But without warning he saw Fiona bolt out of the hotel by herself with no provisional government escort. Cabal immediately set out to follow her. She headed directly to the Hôtel Continental and went inside. As no one was following her, Cabal as per his instructions, stayed outside. *Why did she rush to get here? At least she's safe inside.*

The so-called Bennett was headed to the Hôtel de Crillon. *I must be able to see the door Murphy will leave by. If he leaves at the usual time, I don't need to do anything, but if he leaves early, I need to make sure he spots me to get led on a wild goose chase. We can't afford for Murphy to arrive early, like before. I'll pick a spot between the Crillon and the Continental that Murphy will pass. This plan is foolproof. Poor little George Murphy, this time we're going to kill his real girlfriend, messy like, and make sure he gets blamed for it. Why am I laughing? These capitalists make me sick. Anything we do to hurt them makes the world a better place. Finally I feel good about having to miss the whore on the Champs-Élysées. Now the landowning bitch will get what she deserves.*

Bennett turned onto Boulevard des Malesherbes. He glanced behind his shoulder and choked. *Who is following me? It's McDermott's MI5 friend. If I'm caught, it will blow the whole operation. Murphy and his slut will walk away free.* He felt for the Nagant revolver under his jacket. Got a firm grip on it. He grabbed a woman coming in the opposite direction and held her in front of him. She screamed and screamed and screamed. He drew the gun, leveled it at Sanders and fired. Sanders collapsed. Bennett dropped the woman and ran but had barely gone five feet when the bullet that struck him from behind came out through his chest with a thick spray of blood. He fell to the ground.

ൻ

After lunch Murphy returned to the Hôtel de Crillon, where he tried to catch up on his invoices. The gunshots from Sanders and Bennett were too far away for him to hear. *What can I say to Fiona at dinner? She's so hardheaded and in disregard of her own personal safety. It's like she wants to die for Ireland to cleanse her soul. How can I convince her that her soul doesn't need cleansing, and her being killed by Russians will not advance the Irish cause one iota? In order to bring her to the United States, I'd have to be relieved from active duty in the army and leave the peace delegation, but it's a price I'm willing to pay. It's so strange. When I first joined the delegation, I doubted I was up to the task, while now, I can't picture myself doing anything else.*

Madame Hardy came into the room and said there was a newspaper reporter, Monsieur Durand there to see him.

Murphy stood, his hands limp at his sides. "Show him in."

When Durand entered, he said, "Thank you for seeing me."

"Okay, tell me what this is about. You've never approached me this conventionally before."

"Please save those thoughts for some other time. When I took your photo with Mademoiselle McDermott the other evening, you suggested the anonymous tips I was receiving were predating the events they described."

"Yes, I did."

"Look at this. It was left at my office." He handed Murphy an envelope with a sheet of paper in it. Murphy took the paper out and read it.

PRESS RELEASE

Lieutenant George Murphy of the American peace delegation who has been a known suspect in several crimes, was arrested last evening in his hotel room at the Hôtel Continental for the brutal murder of Mademoiselle Fiona McDermott, a beautiful and charming member of the Irish Provisional Government peace delegation. Her nude body, which was found in the room with him, was savagely beaten and stabbed with a United States Army 1918 model fighting knife, which is not available to anyone other than American soldiers. The handle of the knife is equipped with brass knuckles which were used to beat the victim. Her body had multiple fractures, and her face was unrecognizable. The hotel where this occurred is the headquarters of the unofficial Ukrainian delegation. Murphy himself got his job with the American delegation through the intervention of Congressman James Hamill, the counsel to the Ukrainian delegation. Hamill also has his office in that hotel. Police responded to the hotel room after receiving reports of screams. Mademoiselle McDermott had previously been shot and wounded by a man who was seen with Murphy in a bar before the incident.

Durand paced around the room. "I may not be a prince among men, but something like this, there is no way I will be a party to it. I hope it is not too late to prevent it."

Murphy blurted out, "I have to make a phone call." He picked up the phone and asked the operator to ring the Grand Hôtel.

A woman answered. "Allo, Grand Hôtel."

Murphy was almost shouting. "This is Lieutenant Murphy of the American peace delegation. I need to get an urgent message to Mademoiselle Fiona McDermott."

"She has already been notified of your injury, lieutenant, and that you need her to come to the Hôtel Continental. I'm surprised she hasn't arrived there yet."

"When did she leave?"

"About an hour ago, and it shouldn't take long to walk from here to the Hôtel Continental."

CHAPTER XXIV

AS SOON AS Fiona entered the Hôtel Continental, she was approached by a short woman with an eastern European accent. "Good afternoon Miss McDermott, I am Oksana Andruko from the Ukrainian delegation. I will escort you up to Lieutenant Murphy's room. One of the men from our delegation was able to help him there after he fell."

Fiona clutched her throat. "Where did he fall?"

She inclined her head toward the entrance. "On the front steps coming into the hotel."

"Thank you, Miss Andruko. How did he fall? What leg did he fall on? Was it the one still holding shrapnel?"

The woman was stiff. "I believe it was. That is why it gave out on the step."

Fiona moved her mouth close to the woman's ear. "Has the hotel physician been to see him yet?"

Andruko held up her hand. "No, Lieutenant Murphy wanted to speak with you before deciding if it's necessary. He suspected it was broken but was not sure."

Fiona stopped short. "Broken? You don't wait to call a doctor for something so serious. Why has the hotel not done anything?"

The short woman took her time. "You know how those men from the trenches are. He wants to see you, mademoiselle, before he does anything else."

"George has a phone in his room. Why didn't he call me himself?"

"Because he was not in his room. He was still in the lobby when he asked me to call you." They got on the elevator and proceeded to Murphy's room.

Miss Andruko knocked in what appeared to be a pattern: knock and a pause followed by two rapid knocks. "I don't want to startle him. I believe the door is unlocked. Let us see." She opened the door and held it for Fiona. Fiona could see a shape in the bed but could not make out any face or features. They entered the room. As soon as Miss Andruko closed the door behind them, the figure sprang out of the bed and pressed a funny smelling cloth over Fiona's face. Andruko grabbed her from behind. The last thing Fiona realized before she passed out was the figure who jumped from the bed was the man she knew as Herr Ostomeyer.

&

Murphy rushed toward the Hôtel Continental. *Calling the police right away would destroy the Bolsheviks' scheme, but it would not save Fiona. She left the Grand Hôtel over an hour ago. She must already be at the Continental. If the police respond, the conspirators will kill her. They'd have nothing to lose. They already killed Angeline. There's no way out of it. I must get into the room before they realize I'm on to their plan.*

Murphy had told Richard to wait one hour before calling Commissaire Trudeau and General Harts. He asked Durand to wait with Richard, but Durand insisted on following him to the Hôtel Continental. Murphy shrugged. *Not surprising. He is a reporter after all. It doesn't bother me. I haven't felt this coldness since I was on the battlefield. It's like all emotion has been drained out of me and replaced with focus. Must be the adrenaline.*

When they were about half a block from the Continental Murphy turned to Durand. "You need to drop back a little. If they have a lookout, and he sees us together, they'll know the jig's up."

Durand continued walking. "Okay, but I'm going in after you."

"Fine, but keep your distance. Remember I have to look like I don't know what's going on, like I'm about to blunder into their trap." *None of this would be necessary if I'd told Fiona about the danger at the Hôtel Continental right away. Why wait until tonight? Push the thought out your head, George. Focus!*

Durand hung back as Murphy turned the corner onto Rue de Castiglione. He entered the lobby. *Nothing looks suspicious.* But someone spotted him. The mystery man stayed out of sight but picked up the house phone, rang the room once, and hung up.

Murphy took the elevator to his floor. He approached the door to his room. *Be quiet, quiet, quiet.* He shoved the key into the lock and flung the door open only to be cracked on the head with a baton.

⁂

Sergent Cabal saw Murphy enter the hotel. *Why did McDermott rush so if Murphy wasn't even here yet? But wait. Who's coming out now? It's the mystery man in the photograph. I'm sure of it. What to do?* He went to the nearest police call-box, opened it with his key and picked up the receiver. "This is Sergent Cabal of the Préfecture. I've just spotted the chief suspect in the DuBois murder. He left the Hôtel Continental on foot, turned north on Rue de Castiglione and moved west on Rue de Mont Thabor. He is tall and wearing a dark gray suit with a red and light blue tie. Hair is brown, age about thirty-six. He may be armed and dangerous, approach cautiously." *Now what? Do I stay on post or pursue the mystery man? He's already left the hotel so he's no immediate threat to Mademoiselle McDermott, but if he stays free, he will be. Better to go after him. With all the traffic and pedestrians it would be easy for him to escape if he realizes he's being followed. With this street lighting it's better to keep track of him from a distance until the dispatched police units catch up.*

⁂

In his hotel room Murphy pretended he was still unconscious. The Bolsheviks shoved him on the bed in a half sitting position with his left shoulder on a pillow and his right one against the headboard, his hands tied behind his back. *I've blown it. It's all over. They've got me. They have Fiona. They will kill her. I can't stop them now. Can I? Why did I burst in here? Why was I so stupid, stupid, stupid? The*

French police might have stopped this, if I'd called them. I can't reach my gun. They've probably found it anyway. He couldn't see much other than Fiona on the other side of the bed, naked. *How can I ignore what they're saying, especially the woman?* "You can have some fun now, Boris."

Ostomeyer said nothing. He just smiled, so gruesome. He kissed the fighting knife. "Now for some payback."

Murphy lay still. *How long can I keep pretending?* Despite his tied wrists he could move his fingers. *Is my service weapon still behind the headboard? Did they find it? Do they know there's an opening at the bottom? Can I get my hands underneath it? Do I have enough time? How far away are they, six feet? How much time do I need? Too much!*

Ostomeyer slid the fighting knife with brass knuckles onto his right hand. He looked her up and down.

It's now or never. God help us, please. Murphy rolled to his left, and brought his hands up behind the headboard. The gun was there. It was there. He ripped it out, tape and all, but there was no round in the chamber to fire.

The woman shouted to Ostomeyer. "Stop him. Stop him."

Ostomeyer flew at Murphy with the brass knuckles of the fighting knife. Murphy rolled off the bed as the handle of the knife smashed into his shoulder. He landed on his stomach. Ostomeyer ran around the bed to use the knife on him. He was closing in when Murphy swung his legs and swept Ostomeyer's feet from under him. He came crashing hard on the floor next to Murphy. This bought a few seconds. The woman came up behind Ostomeyer, his baton now in her hand. Murphy squeezed the automatic pistol against his back to hold the slide and pressed the gun forward. Once he pulled the weapon away from his body, the slide snapped back and pushed a cartridge into the chamber. Murphy fired backwards at the woman.

The gun was a .45 automatic, so, dead or alive, she was slammed back against the wall of the hotel room by the large bullet. This was enough to revive Ostomeyer. He snatched the pistol from Murphy's bound hands, pointed it at Murphy and pulled the trigger. Nothing. He threw the gun on the floor with a grunt, and reached for his knife. Murphy, even with his hands tied, was able to grab the gun from the floor behind him and squeeze the back of the handle tightly enough to depress the pistol grip safety. This time the gun fired, and Ostomeyer was blown away by its force.

Murphy dropped the pistol to the floor. As soon as he released the handle, the safety reset itself. He stood and used his bound hands to pull the bedspread over Fiona. He tried but could not wake her. He put his ear to her mouth and nose. *Good, her breathing is normal.*

After opening the door he sat back on the bed with his bound hands visible.

Sergent Cabal stayed a full block behind the mystery man, who was moving quickly. As he approached an apartment on Rue Greffulhe, a light came on in one of the units in the building. There was a noise.

It was a gunshot. It came from there. He drew his weapon and rushed into the building and up the stairs. The door to the apartment was still open, and the mystery man was lying on the floor with a bullet hole right between his eyes. There was a window open in the back of the apartment. Cabal ran to it in time to see a figure reach the ground in the courtyard and run out to the street carrying something. Cabal turned back to the interior of the apartment, which looked like a war room with maps, charts, and schedules. Notebooks were everywhere as well as different forms of identification with multiple names for the same people.

In the doorway stood a group of people with horrified expressions. Cabal looked them over. "I am from the Préfecture de Police. Is one of you the concierge? A woman stepped out from the group. "I will need to use your telephone. No one is to enter the apartment."

CHAPTER XXV

WHEN THE POLICE arrived at Murphy's room, his tied hands were visible. After they were undone he found his Orders to Carry a Firearm and presented the documents to the police. Both Bolsheviks were dead. Neither of them had any identification. Lieutenant Coderre arrived in response to Richard's call. He advised the other officers that Murphy was working in conjunction with the French police.

Murphy and Fiona were taken to the Hospital Hôtel-Dieu on Île de la Cite. Fiona had no damage other than the aftereffects of the chloroform. Murphy suffered a concussion from Ostomeyer's baton and a hematoma on his shoulder from the brass knuckles. The emergency physician wanted them kept overnight in light of the violent nature of their injuries.

The next morning, as Murphy and Fiona were getting ready to leave, a British officer approached them. "Miss McDermott, Lieutenant Murphy." It was Colonel Johnson whom Fiona had met at the Majestic Hôtel.

She greeted him. "Good morning, colonel. Let me introduce Lieutenant George Murphy, who works with the American delegation." She turned to Murphy. "George, this is Colonel Johnson, the head of security for the British delegation."

George extended his hand. The colonel took it and gestured to a door. "If you have time, there is someone in the next room who would like to see you."

Inside Captain Ted Sanders was covered in bandages, lying in bed, and breathing with an oxygen mask. Johnson led them over to the bed. "Captain Sanders encountered the man you knew as Major Bennett on the street yesterday. Sanders recognized him from when Miss McDermott pointed him out at the Hôtel Majestic the day he followed her from the Metro station. They both shot at each other. Sanders here was hit in the left lung. Excuse him if his speech is a little weak. Bennett's wound was fatal."

Fiona grasped Sanders's right hand in both of hers. "How are you feeling, Ted?"

He pushed the mask aside. His voice was weak. "Not bad, considering everything." He coughed. "It's more than made up for by catching up with your attacker. Of course I seem to be one step behind Lieutenant Murphy. I got one. He got two."

Murphy patted him on the shoulder. "Don't belittle yourself. Retuning fire with a bullet in your lung requires a special kind of man, especially accurate fire that takes out the felon and nobody else on a crowded street."

Fiona was tearing up. "You're both my heroes. I can't imagine how a girl with my background could have such noble protectors."

Murphy rubbed her back. "You're well past that part of your background. Once the story about what happened last night hits the newspapers it will undoubtedly be picked up by the Irish press, and you will be more of a star there than you already are."

Johnson got them all seated. "Bennett's real name was Boris Markoff. He lived in Liverpool for ten years, working on the docks before going back to Russia. A native of Liverpool might not have been fooled by his accent, but I don't doubt he would fool an American. While he was in Liverpool, he got in enough brawls that his photograph and fingerprints were on file."

Murphy grinned. "I confess to not being able to tell a Liverpool accent from a London one."

The colonel slid his chair back so he could face all of them. "More important, right after Lieutenant Murphy entered the Hôtel Continental, the French police officer following Miss McDermott spotted your mystery man leaving. He followed him to an apartment in the Eighth Arondisement where the man was shot and killed by a person still unknown. The apartment is a treasure trove of intelligence about what the Bolsheviks were doing here. Unfortunately the Deuxième Bureau, French intelligence, has taken it over from the police, so it might be a while before the rest of us learn anything." He pointed to a paper on his bedside table. "I guess you haven't seen this morning's *Paris Aujourd'hui.*" He handed it to Murphy, who read it aloud.

American Lieutenant Foils Bolshevik Assassins

By Henri Durand

> American Army Lieutenant George Murphy singlehandedly killed two hard-core Russian Bolshevik assassins last night at the Hôtel Continental. Mademoiselle Fiona McDermott, a member of the unrecognized delegation sent here by the provisional Irish government, was saved by Murphy, who was advised of the murder plot by this reporter. Murphy suffered a wound to his own head from a baton and to his shoulder from brass knuckles. Mademoiselle McDermott was knocked out with chloroform and stripped of her clothing. Both are recovering at the Hospital Hôtel-Dieu.

The American delegation sent a car and driver for Murphy and Fiona. They first dropped Fiona off at the Grand Hôtel, and the driver waited outside while Murphy walked Fiona inside. Applause broke out as they entered the lobby, and half the people in the room rushed to congratulate them, including Sean O'Kelly. He shook Murphy's hand. "Thank you for bringing the star of our night back safely."

Murphy looked at his feet. "There was no choice to be made. It had to be done."

O'Kelly put his hand on his shoulder and looked him straight in the eye. "Don't fool yourself. It takes real courage to walk into what he knows is a death trap hoping he can reach the gun he hid inside."

Murphy straightened back up. "One thing I learned in the trenches is you often don't experience fear when you're caught up in a dangerous situation. It doesn't hit you until later. I'm more nervous now than I was when I walked in the room."

O'Kelly nodded. "That may be true, but it doesn't diminish your bravery."

❧

Murphy's return to the Hôtel Continental did not spark applause. The incident had occurred there, and many people had heard the shots themselves. A number of them came over to shake his hand. One of them was Congressman Hamill, who took him aside. "I feel like I'm the catalyst who set this whole thing up. I inadvertently made you a target by helping you get your job, and I made Miss McDermott one by introducing the two of you."

"If that's the case you might as well blame General Harts too for moving me to this hotel, or Mr. O'Kelly for having me take Fiona to lunch at the Hôtel de Crillon. The truth is you all did the right thing. Moral people can't help it if hoodlums attempt to twist good deeds into something else."

"Thank you, that makes me feel better. In the end the assassins' plot appears to have done them more harm than good. It will not bring anyone in Ireland to their side and will drive many away. As far as the Ukraine is concerned, we're not making much progress anyway."

Murphy rechecked into the hotel. His original room was a crime scene. When he opened the door to his new accommodations, he stood there wide-eyed. A spacious suite with a view of the Eiffel Tower greeted him. He called the desk. "I think there's been a mistake. I'm in a grand suite, and my original room was a simple one."

A gallic voice responded, "Non. There is no mistake, monsieur."

Murphy was babbling. "But how much will the American delegation be charged for this? I'm not a senior official."

"Monsieur, there is no additional charge. The upgrade is… how do you say? Complimentary. Merci for protecting the reputation of our hotel. We could not have a delegate to the peace conference, even an unofficial one, murdered on our premises."

There was even a bottle of champagne waiting for him. *If only Fiona could be here to share it. I have to talk with her. We couldn't do so after the shooting. Is she okay emotionally? We were still on a high wire when I left the Grand Hôtel. It's like we're on some different plane that I don't understand, but now, I'm exhausted. I've got to take a nap.*

When he awoke, he dressed and went to the lobby. His head was spinning so he found an out-of-the-way chair and flopped into it. There was a voice behind him. "Translating invoices must be keeping you busy." It was Major Muller standing behind him.

Murphy turned in his seat. "I haven't had much time for that lately, but I do owe you an apology."

Muller walked to the front of the chair. "It's a relief to hear. For weeks everyone has been telling us that we Germans are the only ones who have anything to apologize for."

Murphy adjusted his position to face him. "Look, if I had my way, you would be included in the negotiations, so would Ireland, the Ukraine, Armenia, Egypt and Indo-China. It would be better to talk about our differences now than to fight about them later, but no one's asking me. Russia is an entirely different problem, since it is still not clear who does speak on behalf of the Russian people, and I'm not in the mood to parley with Bolsheviks right now."

"But you are not a delegate."

"No, but more to the point, you were right all along. You were not the source of Fiona's and my problems."

"Thank you. Whatever your confusion, you managed a great feat once you understood the real situation." Muller patted his shoulder and left smiling.

⁂

After lunch Murphy tried telephoning Fiona, but there was no answer. He decided to walk to her hotel. He didn't see her in the lobby, asked the clerk to ring her room and was told she had left word she would be at the café at Place de la Madeleine. He found her sitting at a table toward the back, still wearing the same clothes she had put back on that morning. She spotted him but lowered her eyes. "Surprise, surprise, you found me."

"Isn't that a good thing?"

She lifted only her head. "It is. I would have been disappointed if you hadn't, but it doesn't mean I'm ready to talk."

He plunked himself into a chair. "Okay, I'll deliver a monologue."

She started squirming. "George, I don't mean I can't talk at all. I just can't talk about what happened last night. Yes, I could put on an act for you and Ted and Colonel

Johnson at the hospital, but it's not the same as reliving everything that happened."

He looked around. *How can I calm her*? "Do you mind if I order a carafe of red wine?"

She shrugged. "Eh."

He placed the order and turned to her. "I suspect Captain Sanders will have to go back to England to recuperate. A gunshot wound to the lung will take a while to heal."

She stopped her wiggling. "Thank God the bullet didn't strike his heart, but my thoughts are elsewhere. Have you been following the situation in Ireland?"

"I've seen the Irish Parliament has declared Ireland free and demanded the British leave."

Fiona sat still. "That much has appeared in the international press. What you don't see there is the fighting has already started. The IRA has ambushed munitions shipments and killed the armed escorts. Open warfare is what it is becoming. I don't know what we can do here anymore."

"What can you do there?"

She moved closer and kept her voice low. "I would not make much of a soldier. Concealing bombs is not my style, nor could I ever get away with it. I'm too well known to sneak past anyone unnoticed. Better for me to be where they do want me to be noticed, like at rallies or speeches. It's a strange type of war where the governmental institutions the British consider rebellious are left alone, but there's open gunfire on the highway."

The wine arrived and Murphy poured them each a glass. "How safe is your farm?"

"Probably pretty safe. It's not likely they'll try anything stupid again. I suspect someone tried unsuccessfully to call off the sniper, once they learned there would be an American army officer in the car. They didn't expect you to show up when they were making their plans. Also the notoriety we're both getting now would generate too much bad press. Finally everyone wants the economy to keep functioning. Of course nothing can be ruled out for certain."

"What do you want to do?"

She huffed. "Now, if I knew that, I wouldn't have come over here and had you find me sitting in a corner by myself, would I? At least I can walk alone now without having to worry about getting shot."

Murphy looked at the ceiling. *Better not to get her going again.* "What are you options?"

She sat up to the table. "I can stay here and keep doing what I'm doing. It appears to be safe now since my assailants were eliminated by a combination of you, Ted Sanders, and an unknown gunman. While our delegation will never be seated at the conference, I can still be a spokesman for Ireland's quest for freedom." She forced a smile. "As people here begin reading about more and more ambushes, they will need someone to make clear what it's all about. I could go back to Ireland and do the same thing in Dublin or Cork or Galway. So far the British authorities have been trying to avoid open violence against political activists. Will it change? I don't know." Her voice faded.

"You didn't mention coming to the United States." He closed his eyes. *Am I pushing too hard?*

She put her hand on his arm. "Oh George, I am glad you still think that way. I'm not as convinced as I once was that I need to be a martyr. If fact, after what happened in the hotel room, I dread the possibility. Getting through it has made me lose my fear of other people's opinions about you and me being together, but my commitment to Irish freedom has not faded. I'm not abandoning the cause. One way or the other, I have to see this through to the end. I truly hope you can see that!"

CHAPTER XXVI

WHEN MURPHY REPORTED to General Harts's office the following morning, he was shown right in. The general stood and offered Murphy his hand, something he hadn't done before. "You look good for what you've been through."

"Thank you, sir. Other than getting whacked on the head and shoulder, I wasn't hurt."

"But you brought things to a conclusion, reams of investigation resolved in one turbulent encounter, and I'm delighted to see you back here in good health, captain."

Murphy's eyes widened. "Captain?"

"Yes, you've been promoted. Take these." The general handed him his railroad track insignia. "You can put them on, if you want, but I suspect you might want your Irish lady friend to do it for you."

"Yes, sir. Thank you, sir. I would."

"Now I need you to tell me what happened, the full story."

Murphy took the seat the general offered and went

through everything that happened after their last meeting, Henri Durand's showing him the premature press release, Murphy's walking into the hotel room expecting to be able to make a quick grab for the gun, his being klonked on the head with a baton and his waking up within reach of the gun and thereafter.

Harts's gaze stayed focused on Murphy. "It's extraordinary. What's being done with your service weapon?"

"The French police have taken custody of it. They want to test fire it and compare the signatures on the bullets with the ones taken from the Bolsheviks' bodies."

"A standard procedure to verify there wasn't a second gun involved. Once they return it you can put it back under lock and key at the Hôtel de Crillon. What are your plans for now?"

"To go back and translate my invoices. I never realized how relaxing it could be."

"Your superiors at the peace delegation would probably be grateful. They think I have already taken up too much of your time."

Murphy hesitated. *What did he mean by "would probably be grateful?"* "It was for a good cause." He squirmed. "I know what happened in the hotel room, but not much else."

The general rested back and folded his hands on his chest. "We know who the two Bolsheviks you shot were. The short woman who called herself Oksana Andruko was Klavdiya Vasiliev, and the man who called himself Herr Ostomeyer was Konstantin Morozov. He had lived in Germany for fifteen years which was why he was able to impersonate a German to Miss McDermott. Combined with what MI5 found out about Boris Markoff, also known as Major Bennett, that information tells us a lot. This was an elite team. Klavdiya Vasiliev was one of the Soviets' top resource managers. It's not easy to find agents with good backgrounds to impersonate Germans and British. The loss will be a big drain on Bolshevik resources."

"What about Angeline, Natasha?"

"The fact that she was not a member of that team was what got Ivan Sorokin, better known as your mystery man, killed. Angeline, Natasha, was a precious asset of a loosely allied action group, more political than treacherous. It was Klavdiya Vasiliev who wanted to borrow her to make contact with you as Angeline DuBois for this operation. In addition to discrediting the Ukraine, the Vasiliev woman wanted Angeline's death to cripple a rival operations team she expected to be competing with in the future for status within the new government. Angeline's team leader agreed to the request, not expecting such betrayal."

Murphy stared across the desk. "I would never have expected the Bolsheviks to be turning on each other. Some things I can figure out for myself. Ivan, the mystery man, made sure I spotted him at Angeline's funeral to keep me believing he was German. The episode in Strasbourg served two purposes. It helped discredit me and it gave further reason to believe the mystery man was German, since he used German marks. What do we know about the man who shot him, the team leader?"

"*We* don't know much. Most of what we're getting has to come from the Deuxième Bureau, and they're giving it up bit by bit. If your concern is he might present a risk, you can let it go. Not only will he want to get as far away as possible as soon as possible, but his team does not have a reputation for resorting to violence. Blackmail and misinformation yes, but not assassination. It took the murder of his one of own most valuable agents by a fellow comrade to make him kill. I know it's still early for you to get your thoughts together, but it was quite a feat you accomplished, entering a closed room unarmed and managing to liquidate two professional operatives from a trained espionage unit. You may get put up for another medal, and don't be surprised if the French government includes the Legion of Honor."

As he left the general's office Murphy thought he had not done too badly for a guy who thought Paris was too much for him.

Murphy walked to the café on Rue Rouget de Lisle to meet Claude for lunch. He arrived and was greeted by Count Orlofsky. "I have to commend you for your actions in disposing of the two Bolsheviks and saving Miss McDermott, but I can't understand how you ever let her walk into the hotel in the first place. You knew that was where the trap would most likely be."

Murphy dropped his head. "I agree it was stupid on my part not to tell Fiona sooner. We had planned to have dinner together that evening, which was when I was going to tell her about your warning. It never occurred to me the Bolsheviks would lure her there beforehand."

Orlofsky reached up and patted his arm. "We all make mistakes, but you fixed yours and did even more. Miss McDermott is not the only one made safe by your actions.

There are many other people who were at risk from these Bolsheviks, who are not any longer. Tell me, the woman you killed in the hotel room, was she the one who interrupted us here about the Bolsheviks' making peace with Germany?"

"It was the same one." Claude arrived, and Murphy excused himself as they took an out-of-the-way table.

Claude was out of breath. "Mon ami, what should I say? What you did was incroyable."

"I still have trouble absorbing it myself and I'm not the only one. Fiona is in a haze, and she was always the more stoic one."

Claude ordered a carafe of wine. "Being held hostage is terrifying. I understand the man who chloroformed her was the same one who attacked her in the car, the one she stabbed in the neck. Suddenly being at that man's mercy, it does not go easy. You have to give her time."

"I know, but I don't know where she's going to end up emotionally once the time is up. The risks we were facing seemed to bring us closer together. Now that those risks are eliminated, it's like we're drifting apart." The waiter placed the wine and two glasses on the table.

Claude poured the glasses and slid one over to Murphy. "George, Fiona will not turn away from you. You've held her hand through crisis after crisis. You went to Ireland with her for her father's funeral. You defended her there. Finally, nothing can match what happened at the Hôtel Continental. Don't think for a moment she could come out of it and behave like nothing had happened. Don't push her. Let her go at her own pace."

Fiona went back to the Hospital Hôtel-Dieu to visit Ted Sanders. He was asleep when she arrived, so she sat back in the chair and closed her eyes. *What can I do now? What happened to me? I've been accosted before, but I've never come this close to death. Herr Ostomeyer, or whatever his name was, could have stuck the knife in me anytime he wanted. I cringe just thinking of him taking my clothes off. Thank God I was unconscious. Even at Madame Yvette's I never felt so demeaned, drugged and naked with a creep ready to mutilate me with a gruesome knife. When I thought of dying for Ireland, I never thought of it that way. Do I still have the courage to go forward?*

Her thoughts were interrupted. "Fiona, Fiona, did you fall asleep?" Ted's voice was raspy.

"I did not. I was lost in my thoughts." She roused herself.

He tried sitting up but could manage only an inch or two. "That's not surprising after what you've been through."

"I'm not the one lying in a hospital bed with an oxygen mask on my face and a hole in my lung."

"My encounter didn't require much thinking. I saw Bennett or Markoff or whatever his real name was, draw his pistol, so I drew mine and fired. It was all over except for his bullet. Yours involved prolonged terror."

"For most of which I was unconscious."

"Murphy was awake for most of it. What he did required real courage. He understood exactly what he was walking into and didn't hesitate."

"No he didn't. That's why I feel guilty." She shook her head and looked away.

Sanders was able to sit up a little more. "Guilty about what?"

She composed herself. "I don't think I can ever live up to whatever he must believe our life together would be like."

He managed to roll to face her. "In the past I told you not to underestimate yourself, but now I say don't underestimate him either. Anyone who went through what he did for you is not expecting to spend the rest of his life sipping gin and tonics and lounging in the garden on your farm."

"If you mean like my father did, I know." She even chuckled a little.

"Yes, you know that but how much else do you know? You obviously expect him to give up on you at some point. Where and when would that point be, if not when it was most likely to cost him his life?"

"It would be when everyday drudgery sets in. George is far too noble to give up in the middle of a violent confrontation, but how about when it's all done? Could he settle down in the end with someone with my background and live peacefully ever after?"

Sanders sat full up in the bed and pulled his oxygen mask down. "It would be easy for me to say no and court you myself, but it would be dishonest. He's not going to give up. But be practical. Over the next three to five years no one is going to be relaxing over gin and tonics in your garden. The violence will increase, and everyone knows who you are and where you are. There's not going to be much merriment!"

CHAPTER XXVII

WHEN MURPHY RETURNED to work at the Hôtel de Crillon, he wasn't met with applause, but all work seemed to stop. Everyone wanted to come up and greet him. Richard slapped him on the back, "You won't believe the stack of invoices you have waiting to be translated."

Murphy grinned. "Right now I would love nothing more than to spend my time doing that."

"Don't loosen up too quickly. General Harts wants you over there sometime before now."

"I better go."

He didn't have to wait to be shown in. The secretary pointed back to the office. "Go ahead!"

The general also was abrupt. "I know your delegation would like you back to work on its invoices, but you will have to bear with me a little longer. I need you to do something else."

Murphy stiffened involuntarily but said, "Of course what will it be, sir?"

"The Deuxième Bureau has received a message from the unknown gunman who killed your mystery man."

"A message from the *gunman*! What type of message, sir?"

"He wants to make a trade. The apartment where your mystery man was shot contained a lot of valuable information, but the shooter took the most important items with him."

"What are those, sir?"

"Orders outlining plans for future operations."

No, this can't be happening, just when I thought I was home safe. "He's willing to give those up? Why, sir?"

"He says the plans run contrary to his view of socialist society. They involve large scale killings of civilians."

"But you say he wants to trade. What does he want in exchange?"

The general looked at a folder on his desk. "American troops in Russia took seven Bolshevik prisoners recently during heavy fighting on the upper Tulgas. He wants them released. They are affiliated with his organization."

"Is that a problem?" *Where is this leading?*

Harts closed the folder. "No, that part is easy and has already been approved. The snag is collecting the future operations orders from him."

"How does he propose doing it, sir?"

The general inclined forward, folded his hands on the desk and stared straight into Murphy's face. "He says will place them in your hands only."

Murphy almost fell out of his chair. "Me! Why?"

"He trusts you because you killed Klavdiya Vasiliev. It's like the enemy of my enemy is my friend."

"How am I supposed to go about this?" *Is the general serious?*

"Two days from now, at sunset, you are going to go for a walk. Before you reach your destination, someone will approach you and ask what the weather is in Jersey City now. You will respond it is changing rapidly. The person will bring you to the gunman who will give you the proposed orders."

Murphy held out his open hands. "Can we trust them?"

Harts put the file back in his briefcase. "Probably. There are never any guarantees in these situations, but it would be a lot of trouble to go to just to attack you. You would be a fairly easy target for anyone who did not have to build an elaborate frame-up scheme around it!"

Murphy wanted to get together for dinner with Fiona that evening when he finished work at the Hôtel de Crillon. He couldn't reach her by telephone, so he went back to the Hôtel Continental, bathed, changed into his uniform, put his new insignia in his pocket and walked to the Grand Hôtel. He didn't see Fiona in the lobby.

He approached the front desk. "Would you please ring Mademoiselle McDermott's room?"

The clerk shook his head. "It's not possible, monsieur. Mademoiselle McDermott has checked out."

"Checked out!" *That can't be right. Would she leave without letting me know?* "When was that?"

"This morning, monsieur."

"Do you know where she went?"

The clerk lowered his head. "No, monsieur. Her luggage was loaded into a taxi."

Murphy was at a complete loss. What was she doing? Why didn't she tell him she had to leave? He wandered into the bar where he spotted Sean O'Kelly seated at a table by himself doing some paperwork. Murphy walked over. "Mr. O'Kelly, may we have a word?"

O'Kelly looked up. "Of course, lieutenant. Please have a seat."

Murphy took the red leather chair across the small round mahogany table from O'Kelly. "Actually, it's captain now. I wore my uniform over so Fiona could pin my new insignia on."

Congratulations, it is well deserved, but I fear Fiona won't be able to do it, at least not tonight."

"They're telling me she checked out. Is that true?"

"George, she went back to Ireland."

"Ireland!" He froze. "Why now?"

O'Kelly pushed his paperwork aside. "She said there was nothing more for her to do here now. Whatever our delegation could do has already been done, but I think there's something else."

Murphy was gasping. "Am I that something?"

"She didn't say."

Murphy braced his shoulders. "Do you know where she is in Ireland?"

"I believe she's going first to her farm. Her decision was too sudden to work out any other plans for her. Eventually she will want to go on a speaking tour, but it will take time to organize. The notoriety she received as a result of your incident here has boosted her celebrity status."

"Does it create a risk for her?" He rubbed his forehead with his hand.

"It does, but it also gives her a degree of protection. Were anything bad to happen to her, after all the press coverage, there would be newspaper articles all over western Europe, and maybe even in America. The way things are going, both sides are sensitive to bad press."

"Mr. O'Kelly, I have to go back to Ireland and see her. I would leave right now but I'm under classified orders I can't discuss. Once it is cleared up, I will go."

O'Kelly had an easy smile. "You're right. You should!"

"If you have any contact with her, tell her I will not wear my captain's bars until she pins them on."

"I can get the message to her."

Captain George Murphy accepted he was going to have dinner by himself. Was she running out on him? Was it over? If she wanted to break up, wouldn't she have said so? He wasn't doing as great in Paris as he had thought. This was not what it was like in the trenches. Defeating the enemy was not enough. Fiona needed more than that. Yes, she wanted him to save her, but she did not want him taking over her life. Was that why she was running away? There was nothing he could do about it now. Once he got those clandestine orders, he would take some of the leave time he was due, go to Ireland and let the chips fall where they may, but, one way or the other, he needed an answer from Fiona. He could not accept her disappearance.

❧

At the Hôtel de Crillon the next morning, Richard greeted him. "You look worse than you did after the shooting."

Murphy flopped into his chair and put his head in his hands. "And I feel worse."

"What's up?"

He lifted his head back up. "Fiona went back to Ireland without telling me."

Richard sat in one of the chairs. "Is she coming back?"

"Probably not."

He rested an elbow on Murphy's desk. "Are you going after her?"

Murphy lowered his head again but turned it so he could see Richard. "I would but I can't right now."

"Ah, your secret mission none of us know anything about, except it's with the Bolsheviks again—is that why you can't go after Fiona?"

"It is." He finally sat back. "You know, Richard, I realized I was living in an environment unlike any I ever experienced and unlike any the rest of the world has either. There has never before, in the history of our planet, been a gathering in one city of such a concentration of diplomats and statesmen, gentlemen and cads, thieves and scoundrels, politicians and bureaucrats, heroes and cutthroats, spies and assassins. I knew I could get killed but I just never thought it could put me in this situation, where the light of my life is sitting a mere day's journey away, suffering over what we have been through together, and I can't do a damn thing about it because I have an upcoming business meeting with a murderer."

"George, it's not like you're saying, 'I'll come to see you, honey, when I can find the time.' You are in the middle of a crisis, not of your own making, in a city that is experiencing more crises than anywhere else in the world ever before has."

He thumped his fist on the desk. "How does that help Fiona?"

Richard reached over and patted his arm. "George, Fiona is a highly intelligent woman. She understands the climate here much better than you or I do. She fully comprehends the limitations imposed on you. She went to Ireland knowing that, with a purpose in mind. Trust her judgment. If she were bailing out on you, she would tell you first. She's not one to beat around the bush."

"No she's not!"

Madame Hardy entered the room and announced, "Ambassador White needs to see you."

Murphy headed upstairs to the office. When he entered the ambassador was reviewing a report. "General Harts has given me a full breakdown of your mission. Is it still on the fire for tomorrow?"

"Yes, sir. I haven't heard anything to the contrary."

The ambassador put his paperwork down. "Our intelligence people are expecting it to go well, but it would be healthy to remember these people don't hesitate to kill each other. Who knows what they're capable of, but there's something else I want to discuss. I understand your Irish lady friend went back to Ireland unexpectedly. Do you know what's happening?"

What could he say? "No, sir. If I did not have this mission, I would have asked to take some leave time to find out."

White gave a brief smile. "Once this operation is over, feel free to do so, but now we have to keep our focus on the mission. General Harts will give you your final briefing tomorrow morning. Since this does not relate directly to the peace conference, it is his responsibility, not mine. The intrigue involving you and Miss McDermott was a mixed bag. Even though the two other delegations involved are not officially recognized, they both enjoy considerable political support in the United States. We could not ignore them. This thing tomorrow is a straightforward military intelligence operation with the added factor of being primarily a French matter for the Deuxième Bureau. Had this unknown gunman not asked for you by name, we would probably not even be participating in it."

"I'm still trying to process the fact he did ask for me personally. I'm sorry, sir, but I still don't understand how my participation could possibly be important to them."

"Captain Murphy, the one thing those people are most afraid of is betrayal by those they trust. The reason why you are so significant to them is you were not at the hotel as an agent of anybody. Yes, we had given you some assignments, but they were not why you walked into the room. You could have accomplished whatever political purpose we needed by calling the French police, but once you learned Miss McDermott had been abducted, you didn't. You chose instead to make saving her your principal objective. These Bolsheviks know it and they know anyone who would do something like that is not going to stab them in the back over petty politics. Does that all make sense?"

"It's taking a while to sink into my brain, sir, but I think I get it. They want me because I put saving Fiona ahead of blocking their rival Bolshevik team's plans. To them it makes me the type of person who will not double-cross anyone."

"I think you've got it!"

CHAPTER XXVIII

MURPHY TRIED TO sit still at his desk, but his foot banged into it causing him to grunt and slam his hand down. Only one more day to go before his face-to-face meeting with the mystery man's killer. What could he do in the meantime? Translate invoices? He couldn't concentrate well enough.

Richard called across to him. "You look like a riled up lion in a cage. When is the task of yours I don't know about?"

His foot movement stopped. "Tomorrow evening. I wish it were right now. At least when Fiona was attacked I didn't have time to think about it."

Richard put his papers aside. "I would give you some advice, but since you can't tell me what you're doing, it would be meaningless. I'm glad I'm a civilian hired solely to make travel arrangements. No one is going to come in and say, 'Richard, instead of your usual job, we need you to pick up a bomb today.'"

Murphy snarled, "You still had a rough time with the Germans and their phony checks."

"At least they weren't shooting at me."

"I hope no one will be shooting at me either." He dropped his head and managed to sit still. What about Fiona? Where would she eat? She wouldn't go to a pub in Dungarvan alone. She would probably eat at her farmhouse. Mrs. Fitzpatrick would fix her something nice. What would it be like for him to be there under the open wooden beams in front of the grand fireplace? He could sit back in a large armchair and sip a Jameson's. Would he ever be able to do so again? Was Fiona through with him? Time to put it out of his mind. He was meeting the killer in a few hours, but wasn't he a killer himself? Even if he were to leave aside war deaths, he had shot the two Bolsheviks in the hotel room, but those weren't cold-blooded killings. He had to shoot them to save Fiona. The man he was meeting tomorrow lay in wait for mystery man and put a bullet right between his eyes without further ado. What had Murphy gotten himself into? No, no, he had to stop thinking that way. He was doing what he was supposed to be doing. Getting possession of those orders could save many lives. Were there risks involved? Yes, but nothing like the ones he faced going into the hotel room. He *was* the right person for this job.

⸙

The following morning arrived. On previous occasions when he and General Harts spoke, they were alone. This time there was another man present, a Major Pierce. There was a chart on the wall showing the route from Hôtel

Continental to Sacré-Coeur Basilica. The general pointed at it. "About twenty minutes before sunset you should leave the hotel and walk over to the Jardin des Tuileries. You'll be able to see the sun better from there. Once it starts to set, head back toward the hotel and go north on Rue de Castiglione. You will follow this route toward Sacré-Coeur Basilica. You have a map, so you will not need to remember it all. You probably won't get far before someone approaches you. You're easy to recognize. Your picture has been in the paper several times. Make sure whoever approaches you has the correct introductory phrase. We can't follow you, but we can follow this route ten to fifteen minutes after you and we will have stationary lookouts at various points, mostly indoors, along it. Of course whoever intercepts you may divert you to another route."

Murphy was barely managing to control his fidgeting. "I believe I can do it, sir, and unless anyone stops me, I will get those documents back to you. Excuse me for asking, but what else might happen?"

The general returned to his chair. "I won't kid you, captain, we simply don't know. Do we believe this guy wants to cooperate? Yes! Can we be one hundred percent sure? No! At this point you are an unlikely target after your rescue of Miss McDermott. It would be hard to make you look like a bad guy now, and our contact, at least, appears to be grateful for your eliminating his competition. The truth is you're going over the top again, quietly, like when you were a forward observer for the field artillery. Maybe you'll run into real trouble, probably not."

"What should I do once I get the documents?"

"George, I think you're going to be okay. Whoever he

is, he's already got his prisoners released. I believe he does want us to have these documents. Right now he's more concerned with interference from rival Bolsheviks than from us. Remember he's still smarting over Angeline, Natasha's murder by people he thought were his allies. I'm sure you understand you can't be armed. It would be likely to set things off. Once you have the documents, get back on the route and head back toward the Hôtel Continental. Our people should be able to pick you out pretty quickly.

"Major Pierce here has a briefcase for you." Pierce held it up.

Harts tilted his head toward it. "You will note, in addition to the handles, there is a leather loop, like at the top of a dog leash. Stick your hand through it before grabbing the handles. It will make it hard for anyone to snatch the case from you."

Murphy's face snapped back toward the general. "Who would do that? Certainly not the people who had just given the documents to me."

Harts motioned his hand in a calming fashion. "If you are going to be dealing with the Bolsheviks you should know the rivalry we see, in Paris between different communist organizations, goes all the way up to the top."

"So, there are people here who believe they are the rightful heirs, not just of those orders, but also of the missions they direct."

The general held up a hand. "Exactly. Now Major Pierce has something to say."

Pierce stood up and walked to the chart. "Remember, your rendezvous point back with us is the Hôtel Continental. If you can get back to it using the same route, do so.

We will find you there. If you can't go that way, get to the hotel however you can!"

❧

Murphy wasn't hungry but he knew he had to keep his strength up, so he had a late lunch. He went to a café and ordered smoked salmon salad with a glass of burgundy and watched the other customers. What were they doing here? Were they tourists enjoying an afternoon in Paris? Were they businesspeople discussing commerce over a late lunch? Were they diplomats from the conference, or were they secret foreign agents involved in the same type of subterfuge he was?

When he got back to his glamorous suite he took off his shoes and lay back on the bed. He was staring at the ceiling while the sun lowered in the sky. He got up, put on his shoes, his tie and his jacket, picked up his new briefcase, made the sign of the cross, opened the door, and walked out.

There was an unobstructed view of the sun from the Tuileries Gardens. For a while, Murphy walked in circles until the lower rim of the sun got near the roofline of the distant buildings. Once the edge dropped below the roofline he headed back past the hotel entrance and continued along Rue de Castiglione. When would someone come up to him and utter the key phrase? Would he be able to pick out the contact before the contact approached him? Once he turned on Place de L'Opera he was close to the Grand Hôtel. Nothing for him there now, not with Fiona back in Ireland. His heart fluttered so much, he almost didn't notice the woman standing directly in front of him until she said in French, "What is the weather like in Jersey City now?"

He almost flubbed his answer. "It is changing rapidly."

The woman had Angeline's big deep brown eyes. "We will go to the Metro station." He followed her. They descended the steps to the platform. A train came. She did not let him get on it. She looked around. No one else had stayed on the platform. They got on the next train. She told him where to sit, sat next to him and nudged him. "Put your briefcase between us." He did. At St. Lazare, when a man approached them, she got up, and the man sat in her seat. After a minute, without a word, he put a large envelope in Murphy's briefcase. At Gare de l'Est, he got off and the woman motioned Murphy to come along behind her. "Go around and get on the next train back to Place de L'Opera. We're done."

Murphy stared into her eyes. "You remind me of someone."

She sniffled. "I know. She was my little sister. Thank you." She hustled away.

Murphy held tight to the briefcase, walked up one stairway and down another to get the train in the opposite direction. When it came, he got on it. At Place de L'Opera he got off. This wasn't so bad after all. He got the documents, and he was still alive. He climbed the staircase to Place de L'Opera. It was dark when he reached the top. He stretched his legs, looked around, and collapsed on the ground!

CHAPTER XXIX

WHERE WAS HE? How long had he been asleep?

The bed was comfortable, but there was a lot of paraphernalia attached to him. His head hurt, and he was dizzy and nauseous. A woman's voice said, "Doctor, Captain Murphy appears to be waking up."

He opened his eyes, and everything was fuzzy. He made out a man in a white lab coat who said, "Captain Murphy, I'm Doctor Cambron. You're here at the Hospital Hôtel-Dieu. You have a nasty fractured skull and cerebral contusion, but we now know you're going to survive. Can you hear me?"

"Y… yes," Murphy sputtered. "What hap… happened?"

"You took a blow to the head. You've been unconscious for four days. You had some bleeding in your brain, but it has stopped. Right now we need you to rest. We'll have to wait to see when your equilibrium comes back." Murphy closed his eyes at the news and fell asleep.

When he woke up again, Major Pierce was seated in the chair.

Murphy's head was too painful to move. "Maj—"

Pierce got to his feet. "Don't strain yourself. How are you feeling?"

"It... hurts... but that means I'm still alive."

"And lucky to be so. You took a nasty blow to the head from a blackjack. Our lookout on the upper floor of the Grand Hôtel spotted you going to the Metro station with a woman at Place de L'Opera. We notified the police who staffed the area. Unfortunately, when you returned, they did not spot the man who attacked you in time to prevent the assault. The guy whacked you across the head, fracturing your skull. The police grabbed him and the documents while you were lying there unconscious. Of course, they gave the documents to the Deuxième Bureau rather than to us, but at least they're in the hands of the good guys now."

"So the... planned at—tacks won't take place."

"Right."

Murphy drifted off again. The next time he woke up, a familiar looking woman sat in the chair, but he couldn't place her. He shifted in the bed and looked at her again. "Mrs. Fitzpatrick?"

"Aye, that it is. I came to Paris to speak to you but, Jesus, Mary, and Joseph, I didn't expect to find you like this! The last episode, the shooting in the hotel room, was all over the newspapers, but not a word about this!"

He tried to stretch his muscles. "It's because it's classified. More important, how is Fiona?"

She closed her eyes a few seconds before starting up again in a low voice. "Not good. I've never seen her like this before. I heard she had a rough time when Mr. McDougal was killed in the Easter Rising, but she didn't come home after that. You know, her father and all. She drinks and sleeps and paces back and forth. She's losing weight. My cousin is looking after her now. I told Fiona I had to visit an old friend who was sick. I couldn't tell her I was coming to see you. I don't think she heard me anyway. I wanted you to come back to Ireland with me, but it can't happen now."

He pushed his back up onto the pillow. "I will go as soon as they'll let me."

"I know. I hope it's not too late."

Murphy was feeling a lot better the next day. He was able to make it as far as one of the chairs when Richard came to see him. "You're out of bed."

"Barely. I'm going to have to do a lot more than this to get to Ireland."

Richard sat in another chair. "Why such a rush?"

Murphy tested his legs, moving them up and down. "Fiona's not doing well. Her housekeeper showed up here from Ireland yesterday and told me Fiona is drinking like she did when her last boyfriend was killed. Mrs. Fitzpatrick thinks the only solution is for me to go to Ireland and talk to her, but I can't even make it out of this room without falling. I told Mrs. Fitzpatrick she could have my suite at the Hôtel Continental while she's here, since I'm not using it."

Richard stood and put his hand on Murphy's shoulder. "George, you're not going to be of use to anyone to all, least of all to Fiona, until you get your health back. A fractured skull with a cerebral contusion is a serious, serious injury. You've only had eight days to recover so far. That's not enough. They didn't think you were going to make it at first, so be happy you're still breathing."

He took a deep breath. "I am, Richard, but I need to do something about Fiona. It sounds like a crisis."

"So is your injury. You would not likely survive a trip to Ireland now. Take it from me. Fiona will be attended to until you are ready."

"How? Even Mrs. Fitzpatrick is no longer there with her."

Richard raised his hand. "Trust me."

Two days later Murphy was feeling a little steadier and tried walking around his room a couple of times. He heard steps and looked toward the door only to see Henri Durand standing there. Murphy allowed himself a grin. "I used to get annoyed when you arrived."

Durand smiled. He was holding a pencil and pad. "See how things, they can change."

"Thank you for your help with the premature press release. Please have a seat." Murphy settled into one himself.

Durand sat across from him. "I had a duty to do so. Our ethics aren't as different from lawyers' as you think. If a man tells a lawyer 'I killed a man yesterday,' the lawyer has to keep it confidential. If the same man said, 'I am going to kill a man tomorrow,' the lawyer would have to report it. Our situation was similar. And the lady, just sit back and let her be brutally murdered? No, no, no. He shook his head back and forth." He threw his hands in the air and sat silent before he looked up. "But what happened to you? Who was the man the police arrested? Was he a Bolshevik?"

Murphy rubbed his neck. "Probably, but I don't know for sure. You're well aware of our involvement with Bolsheviks."

"What was in the briefcase?"

"Classified documents. That's all I can tell you."

"Did they concern Bolsheviks?"

"Probably, considering the environment we were in, but I can't say for sure. I never saw them. I was just a courier."

"Who were they from?"

"I don't know his name."

"Was he a Bolshevik?"

"It's likely, but there's not much more I can tell you."

"Not a problem. Wait until you see the story I can build just from this."

As soon as Durand left, Claude arrived. "Was that Henri Durand I saw leaving?"

Murphy looked up with a grin. "It was."

Claude kept his eyes on the door. "What did he want?"

"To know what happened to me. I didn't tell him anything he couldn't figure out for himself. I wouldn't have gotten to Fiona in time if he hadn't shown me the press release, so I owed him something."

Claude took the seat Murphy offered. "Speaking of Fiona, have you heard anything more?"

"Her housekeeper came all the way from Ireland just to tell me she's not well, and I need to get to her, but the doctors are saying a choppy ferry ride could throw me back into a coma."

Claude threw his head back. "George, do what the

doctors say. You can't accomplish anything by trying to go there in your condition."

Murphy was fading. "I know, but it doesn't stop me from thinking about how miserable she is and I'm not doing a damn thing about it."

~

The next afternoon, Stephen Brown from Murphy's office arrived carrying his uniform.

Murphy pointed at it. "What's that for?"

Stephen stood still. "It's for the ceremony tomorrow?"

Murphy rolled his head to the side. "What ceremony?"

"You're being awarded the Distinguished Service Medal. General Harts is going to present it."

Murphy took the uniform and felt in the pocket. His captain's bars were still there. "I was hoping to get Fiona to pin these on before I wore the uniform again."

"I don't think the general will mind if you leave your first lieutenant's bars on. He understands why, and it's not like you're walking around a military base in your uniform all day."

He hung his head. "I hope I'm not engaging in fantasy in believing she's coming back."

"George, something will happen."

"What time is the ceremony tomorrow?" He looked up.

"Five o'clock in the evening."

CHAPTER XXX

MURPHY SLEPT THROUGH most of the next day, just taking his meals. Around four o'clock he got up and put his uniform on. He felt the captain's bars in his pocket. He looked in the mirror and combed his hair. He was still tired. Congressman and Mrs. Hamill were the first to arrive.

Mrs. Hamill accepted a peck on the cheek from Murphy. "I can't believe how handsome you still look in your uniform after all you've been through. Are they feeding you decently?"

"The food's not as good as at the hotel, but it's better than American hospital food."

Claude arrived next and looked him up and down. "You're looking better every day."

The next arrival was Colonel Johnson from the British delegation who advised them Captain Sanders was back in England and was doing well.

Murphy saw Stephen arrive by himself. "Where's Richard? I thought you two would come together."

Stephen muddled, "Richard? Oh, he had to go out of town, but don't worry, he promised he'd be back in time for the ceremony."

Who should show up next but Henri Durand, with a camera. "I want to get a picture of General Harts pinning the medal on you."

Murphy grinned. "I think you're entitled to it."

Stephen glanced at his watch. It was getting late. It wasn't until almost five twenty when General Harts and Major Pierce came into the room. Pierce brought an American flag on a pole, which he set up in a stand next to the general for the presentation. Harts stood before the group. "I believe we're all ready now." He pointed at Murphy's shoulder. "Captain, you're still wearing your lieutenant's bars!"

"Yes, sir. I was waiting for Fiona to pin the new ones on."

Harts put his hand on Murphy's shoulder. "The reason we were delayed was we were waiting for Mr. Ambrose to arrive. He may have a solution to your problem." At this Murphy saw Richard walk into the room accompanied by Fiona. He couldn't believe how much weight she had lost in just a couple of weeks. Had she stopped eating altogether? He was so used to seeing her in snug clothing. Now her clothes were hanging off, but she was smiling. Mrs. Fitzpatrick followed her in.

For a while no one said anything, but Murphy broke the silence. "Fiona!" She trembled as she hugged him.

Richard was out of breath. "We're sorry to have held everyone up. Fiona and I had to wait for a train from Cherbourg."

Tears filled Fiona's eyes. "I didn't know what had

happened to you. There was nothing in the newspaper about it."

Durand adjusted his camera. "There will be tomorrow."

Murphy reached in his pocket and handed his insignias to Fiona. "Do you know how to do this?"

She panted. "I can do it."

Durand snapped a picture as Fiona pinned them on Murphy's uniform. The she kissed him lightly on the lips.

General Harts stepped forward. "Now we'll do the presentation." Murphy stood at attention while General Harts recited:

"I hereby present the Distinguished Service Medal to Captain George Murphy for sustained heroism and exceptionally meritorious service to the United States of America while serving with the United States Delegation to the Paris Peace Conference of 1919."

Harts pinned the medal on Murphy's jacket and stepped back. Murphy raised his hand in salute and held it until the general returned the salute after which Murphy brought his own hand down. At this both Murphy and the general shook hands while Durand photographed them.

The general smiled and turned to the audience. "Under normal circumstances, this would be when we pass the champagne around, but the doctors told us alcohol is out of the question for Captain Murphy right now. Plus he's tired. The rest of us are going to go for champagne and chocolate, but I think Miss McDermott wants to stay here."

Fiona smiled again. "That I do."

Mrs. Fitzpatrick followed up with, "And I will wait outside so Fiona doesn't have to go back alone. We can both stay in Captain Murphy's suite. There's more than enough room for two women."

When everyone else left Murphy turned to Fiona and smiled. "Hi."

Without saying anything, she hugged him tighter than before placing her lips against his. Finally she stepped back a little but continued to hold his shoulders. "You could have died before I even knew you were injured."

Murphy rubbed her elbows. "I was unconscious. By the time I woke up I was out of the woods, at least as far as dying goes. I was trying to figure out how I could get to you. I guess Richard figured it would be easier to get you here."

"Richard arrived in a chicken truck. He had no trouble getting as far as Dublin, but there was no car waiting for him, like there was for us, to drive to Dungarvan. Fortunately he was able to find someone who had delivered a truckload of chickens to Dublin and was returning to a farm south of me. Richard paid handsomely to ride in the back and arrive covered in feathers. Mrs. Fitzpatrick's cousin was able to get them off his suit. She treated it as a normal occurrence. Someone in her family must raise chickens."

She dropped her hands from his shoulders. "But I was shocked to see him. I expected you might show up at some point, but when Richard came instead of you, I knew something bad happened before he even opened his mouth. I poured my drink down the drain. I asked him to tell me everything. He was considerate enough to start out by saying you had recovered consciousness before he left, and your life was no longer in danger. It was a big relief. He filled me in on some of the details of your mission. What were you thinking getting involved in something like that in the first place?"

He rubbed her arms. "As Richard himself pointed out to me, I'm not a civilian like he is. He can't be ordered to undertake such a mission. I can."

"Oh, George, I knew you wanted me to pin on your new insignia, but I thought you would come to Ireland. Richard said it had to be done for this ceremony, and you were still in no condition to travel. So we set out to come here. I had someone drive us to the ferry in Dublin, so Richard would not have to find another chicken truck, and here we are."

"How long are you going to stay?"

She looked away before answering. "George, I'll stay until you're well enough to get by on your own, but I do have to go back to Ireland. Sean O'Kelly will have no trouble finding enough work for me to do here in the meantime."

"Do you plan on eating while you're at it?"

She pressed her lips together before responding. "I am going to eat, George! You should stop worrying about me and take care of yourself. I've gotten out of the dumps before, and I can do it again. Your injury shocked me enough. I'm not one hundred percent better, but I can function again. Right now you look like you're ready to fall over, so maybe you should lie down before you collapse. I'd help you get your uniform off, but I don't think they would approve here. Do you want me to call a nurse?"

"No, I can take care of it." He didn't. He woke up several hours later, still in his uniform and lying on top of the covers. He called the nurse, who brought him his dinner.

When Murphy awoke again in the morning, Richard was there holding a copy of the day's *Paris Aujourd'hui.* The front page had a photo of Fiona pinning on his captain's bars. Next to the photo was an article.

American Army Officer Receives Medal and Promotion for Daring Undertaking

by Henri Durand

> American army Lieutenant George Murphy was promoted to captain yesterday and awarded the Distinguished Service Medal in a ceremony at the Hospital Hôtel-Dieu. Major General William Wright Harts, American Military Governor of the Paris Region, presided over the ceremony.
>
> The Distinguished Service Medal was awarded after the lieutenant's recent successful completion of a highly secret mission to recover, from Russian Bolshevik agents, classified documents vital to the security of the City of Paris. During the operation Murphy suffered a fractured skull.

After reading the article Murphy folded the paper. "I'm glad Durand switched from trying to make me look like a bad guy to the opposite."

Richard took the paper back. "What he's writing is more accurate now. You pulled off two amazing feats in a short period of time."

Murphy swung his legs onto the floor. "And yet I was more comfortable before them. There were more uncertainties then, but at least Fiona and I were at peace with each other. I don't know what we are now."

ര

Fiona did not show up at the hospital that day. Where was she? It wasn't until the evening of the following day when she arrived, pulled a chair over to the bed and sat near him. She sniffled and didn't say anything for a spell. "I'm sorry it took me so long to get back. There's so much work backed up."

Murphy raised himself to a sitting position. "What would they have done with all the work if you didn't come back from Ireland?"

She made a throw-away gesture with her hand. "I've had three meetings with women's groups—"

"Is that all they're letting you do now? To make you feel safe?"

Fiona stood up, looked down and squeezed her fists. "I'm safe. I'm safe. It's no longer a problem. More than anyone else I have you to thank."

"If it wasn't for me the Bolsheviks might not have gotten to you. They considered me useful."

She sat again. "Oh George, neither you nor I were their real targets. We were just flotsam that got in the way of bigger issues. Maybe that's all we'll ever be."

"Not to each other."

Her hands tightened on her lap. "But I'm not limited to talking only to women. I also met with Egyptian men concerned about the lack of representation at the conference for British territories. They tried to convince me I should visit Egypt to get a firsthand look at their situation."

He lifted his eyebrows. "Egypt?"

"I told them when I got married, I could go there with my husband."

Murphy sat forward on the bed. "Your husband?"

"Oh, George, what was I to say to them? I couldn't say 'Yes, take me there now,' any more than I could say 'You're an old masher. Leave me alone.' I am supposed to be a diplomat after all."

"I'm more interested in your mysterious reference to a husband."

She came over to him and rubbed his arm. "George, you know very well I'm not married."

Murphy covered Fiona's hand with his. "But you said, 'when I got married.'"

"George, I was trying to get them to change the subject back to the peace conference and away from a visit by me to North Africa."

"But you allowed marriage would be a possibility."

Her lips tightened. "Maybe I did. So what?"

"Is it?"

"George, I have to go back to Ireland."

He swung his legs off the bed. "For how long?"

"I don't know how long. At least until home rule is achieved."

"And afterwards?"

"I don't know." She took his hands in hers. "Can you suggest something?"

EPILOGUE

ON JUNE 28, 1919 the Treaty of Versailles which resulted from the Paris Peace Conference was signed in the Hall of Mirrors at Versailles by multiple nations. Although President Woodrow Wilson signed on behalf of the United States, it was never ratified by the United States Senate. In 1921 new treaties were negotiated and ratified between the United States and its World War I adversaries. Even for the nations that did fully adopt it, the Treaty of Versailles proved itself unworkable. Most historians feel its harshness was one of the causes of World War II as well as multiple other conflicts around the globe.

Prior to the signing of the treaty a different event occurred in Dungarvan, County Waterford, Ireland. Captain George Murphy wore his dress blue uniform, so it displayed, not just ribbons but full medals, specifically the Distinguished Service Medal, the Silver Star, the Purple Heart, the Great War Victory Medal and the French Legion of Honor. Equally adorned, much to the delight of the ladies present, was his guest Capitaine Claude Bisset in his French dress blue uniform with double rows of brass buttons and a golden sash tied at the waist. The stage was set. Murphy stood at the altar rail of Saint Mary's Church along with his brother, who had sailed from New York with his parents and sister. Father Edward Murray, arrayed in full vestments, waited with them. The altar boys next to him wore cassocks and surplices. Even in troubled times Ireland was never short of flowers and they flowed over and around the altar.

The power of the organ resounded through the crowded church focusing everyone's attention to the door at the back. The first to enter was Brigid O'Hanlon in her long maid of honor dress. Everyone stood, and Fiona appeared wearing her mother's wedding dress to be escorted to the altar on the arm of Sean O'Kelly.

Murphy agreed to stay in Ireland until home rule was established and changed his status with the army to inactive reserve. Fiona, for her part, agreed once home rule was in place, she would live anywhere Murphy wanted. Since they needed to spend time in Dublin anyway, Murphy joined the Inn of Court there to work on his legal training.

On December 6, 1922, with the establishment of the Irish Free State, home rule finally came to Ireland. For the Ukraine it took much longer. It was not until 1991, with the breakup of the Soviet Union, that it achieved independence, after which it was referred to simply as "Ukraine."

Now that you have finished reading *A Prelude To Versailles,* please consider leaving a review online

ACKNOWLEDGMENTS

I first want to thank my loving wife Marlene, both for her advice and for her patience in putting up with my long hours at the desk, also my wonderful daughter Mary Beth. My fine editors Lisa Poisso, Martha Hayes and Robin Samuels deserve much credit. Praise also goes to my cousins who reviewed the manuscript for me, Arthur McGuire, John McGuire, John Sweeny, Roro Poden, Maeve Ostrowski, Ellen Roumasset and Isabel Milazzo, as well as our dear friends Ed and Renee Vassallo. My Beta Readers were a big help, Clif Flynt, Denise Thompson, Miranda Lukatch, Lynn Snyder, Alfred Maree and Kay Spencer. This is the second excellent cover that has been designed for me by Damonza, thanks to both Damon and Robynne. I especially want to thank two four-legged friends, cocker spaniels, who actually sat with me while I worked, Henry, who has passed on, and Teddy Bear, who's watching me now to make sure I spell his name right.

Made in United States
Orlando, FL
02 February 2024

43192479R00153